BC

'So we agree we don't actually dislike each other, then?'

Far from it. Kate looked at him wordlessly. This was not how any of it was supposed to happen. Her heart tripped. 'Aiden, I…'

'Yes, Kate?' He could see her chest rising and falling more quickly, hear the plaintive little catch in her breathing. And he'd never been more turned on in his life.

He moved closer, put out his hands and closed them on her upper arms.

At his touch, Kate felt the sudden wild dip in her stomach, the violent beating of her heart. She tried to swallow, but it was difficult, raspy. 'I just need some space…'

'You don't…' Aiden applied pressure through his hands, capturing her in one easy movement, aligning her body with his. 'You don't need space, Kate. This is what you need. What we both need—isn't it…?'

Kate felt her legs turn to jelly, her world implode, as his mouth descended on hers swiftly, cutting off any response she might have made.

Aiden felt her lips, soft and giving, his for the taking and he plundered them in a brief hard kiss. 'You still want space?' he husked, breaking away with what little willpower he had left.

Dear Reader

I'm delighted to present my new story, DAREDEVIL AND DR KATE. Once again I have chosen to set a story in the glorious rural district of Mt Pryde in south-east Queensland. For those of you who have read and enjoyed my previous stories centred around the medical practice in Mt Pryde, you'll be pleased to know that familiar characters will be popping up regularly in this new story.

In DAREDEVIL AND DR KATE we meet Kate Preston, the new doctor at the Mt Pryde practice. A widow with two young children, Kate just wants to pull her weight in the medical team and enjoy a settled life with her kids. She doesn't bank on having her safe world rocked off its axis by roguish, *out there* Dr Aiden O'Connor! Kate thinks she can ignore his overtures, but Aiden thinks winning Kate is an enticing challenge—one he can't ignore. It's a bumpy ride—especially when Kate is torn between her role as a mother and her needs as a woman.

I hope you will enjoy DAREDEVIL AND DR KATE.

With warmest wishes

Leah Martyn

DAREDEVIL AND DR KATE

BY
LEAH MARTYN

First published in Great Britain 2012
by Mills & Boon, an imprint of Harlequin (UK) Limited.
Large Print edition 2012
Harlequin (UK) Limited, Eton House,
18-24 Paradise Road, Richmond, Surrey TW9 1SR

ISBN: 978 0 263 22461 0

Harlequin
natural, re ... ıade
from woo ... ging
and manu
environme ... n.

Printed an
by CPI Ar

Leah Martyn loves to create warm, believable characters for the Medical™ Romance series. She is grounded firmly in rural Australia, and the special qualities of the bush are reflected in her stories. For plots and possibilities, she bounces ideas off her husband on their early-morning walks. Browsing in bookshops and buying an armful of new releases is high on her list of enjoyable things to do.

Previous titles by the same author:

WEDDING IN DARLING DOWNS
OUTBACK DOCTOR, ENGLISH BRIDE

These books are also available in eBook format from www.millsandboon.co.uk

For Pam, who is always in my corner
and who always gets the first copy!
Cheers, Pammy

CHAPTER ONE

KATE looked critically at her reflection in the full-length mirror. It was her first day flying solo in her new job at the Mt Pryde surgery and she wanted to look good. More than that, she wanted to *feel* good.

Stepping back from the mirror, she completed her inspection. Her dark pants and fitted pin-striped shirt looked just right. Professional. Her hair was neat, her make-up minimal but perfect.

And why was she preening like a teenager? Impatiently, Kate turned away from the mirror. She was a sole supporting parent with two dependent kids. If that didn't keep her feet on the ground, nothing would. Pushing a wad of tissues into her shoulder bag, she zipped it closed.

'Come on, kids,' Kate called, as she left her bedroom. 'Get your backpacks. We need to go.'

Within a couple of minutes, having done it a thousand times, she'd settled her children into the back seat of her silver-grey Lexus. As she started the engine her stomach began rolling and hitching like a hot-air balloon coming in for a landing. *Don't you cave on me*, she warned the offending stomach silently as she reversed out of the driveway and drove towards the children's primary school.

'Mummy, are you a real doctor?' six-year-old Mia asked as they drove.

Kate bit down on a smile. Her little daughter was so cute, her questions always out of left field. 'Yes, darling. I'm a real doctor. Why do you ask?'

''Cos I found a story book at Grammy's an' the doctor wore a long white coat. You don't wear a long white coat.'

'That's probably a very old story book,' Kate said. 'Doctors don't bother with white coats these days.'

'Mum?' Eight-year-old Luke's voice rang with childish impatience. 'Where can I practise my soccer?'

Kate racked her brains. 'Honey, I don't have an answer to that. Maybe we can find a park nearby, when we've time to look.'

'There's no room in the garden at home,' Luke grumbled. 'I wish we were still out at the farm with Grammy and Pa.'

Don't we all. Kate suppressed a longing. It would have been so easy to move in with her parents and offload some of her responsibilities. But there were no choices here, no shorts cuts. She and the children had to live in town, her job and their schooling demanded it.

And, talking of schools, here they were. Kate pulled neatly into the kerb.

'What if we don't like the school?' Luke asked anxiously as he trundled out of the car.

'You will,' Kate reassured him, helping Mia out of her safety seat. 'Just do your best and you'll be fine.'

With Luke and Mia having been welcomed by their teachers and shown their desks, Kate felt free to leave. It was only a short distance across town to the Mt Pryde Medical Centre. She began to reconnect with her own day. She'd been so fortunate to get this job with hours arranged more or less to fit in with the needs of her children. And with her parents being only twenty kilometres away, her decision to move to south east Queensland seemed a sound one.

Subconsciously, she braced herself as she turned her car into the designated parking space at the rear of the surgery. *Oh, rats!* I shouldn't be feeling this nervous, she berated herself, trying for nonchalance as she crossed to the rear entrance of the building. Like she'd told Luke, she'd do her best and no one could ask for more than that.

Tapping out the security code that would admit her to the building, she made her way inside to what was now her consulting room, feeling a little sliver of pride to see her name, Dr Kate Preston, on the door.

Kate was taking the place of Jo McNeal who had just begun maternity leave. Kate had spent the last week working with her as she'd handed over her patient list. Jo's husband Brady also worked at the practice, along with Angelo Kouras and Aiden O'Connor.

The medical team seemed like a good mix of personalities, Kate thought, arranging her own bits and pieces on the desk. Angelo rather serious, although Kate suspected he had a droll sense of humour bubbling away not too far from the surface. His wife, Penny, was the anaesthetist at the local hospital, and he'd been the longest in the practice.

Then there was Brady. Kate had felt at ease with him at once. 'If you come up against an emergency with the kids at any time and need cover, just yell,' he'd said kindly. 'I know what it's like to be a sole parent and trying to hold down a responsible job.'

He'd gone on then to tell Kate he'd had the care and custody of his infant son before he'd met and married Jo. Now little Andrew was almost three and he and Jo were expecting their own baby in a few weeks.

Then there was Aiden.

Suddenly Kate's throat felt as dry as dust. Meeting Aiden O'Connor had made her feel *flustered* for want of a better word. And an odd awareness that something was missing from her life had begun niggling and wouldn't be ignored.

Damn. Kate moved to open the slatted blind to let in the clear morning light. Out of the blue, she felt her skin heat with just the thought of being in the same workplace as him. Day after day.

Kate began to sift through the mail their receptionist, Vicki, had left on her desk. *Oh, good.* She drew out the envelope containing the X-rays Jo and she had been waiting for. But now, of course, with Jo on leave, all decisions on patient care would be down to Kate. Thoughtfully, she placed the first of the X-ray films on the viewing screen.

She turned at the rat-a-tat on her door. 'It's open.'

'Morning, Kate.' Aiden poked his head in.

Kate felt her composure drain away, her stupid heart bouncing like a trampoline, juggling for space inside her chest. 'Good morning.'

Aiden breezed in and parked himself on the edge of her desk. 'I've been commissioned to tell you coffee's up and to twist your arm if necessary.' He ran teasing blue eyes over her. 'You're not a workaholic, are you, Dr Preston?'

Kate brought her small chin up. 'No more than anyone has to be in a busy practice.' She caught her lower lip between her teeth, exercising gentle pressure, trying anything to sideline her thoughts from savouring the detail of 'Dr Distraction', as she'd begun to call him in her head: the way his charcoal-grey shirt accentuated the broad sweep of his shoulders; the narrow hips in his black jeans; the fact that there was a lean athleticism beneath his well-fitting clothes.

Her gaze connected briefly with his clear blue eyes and flicked higher, lingering on his hair, short, toffee brown, spiked with gold, as if naturally streaked by the sun. She guessed his tan was an all-year-round attribute, enhancing the outdoorsy look of him. Well, that figured. Aiden O'Connor was sports mad according to the practice grapevine. Mountain-climbing, snowboarding and extreme sports positively turned him on—the pursuits Kate had once enjoyed but now had serious reservations about. She released the pressure from her lip and swallowed. O'Connor was possibly the best-looking man she'd ever met. She'd not risked such thinking until now but it was the inescapable truth.

'So, Kate.' Aiden slid off his perch to peer over her shoulder. 'Whose foot do we have here?' He gestured to the skeletal framework thrown up by the X-ray.

'Fifty-four-year-old male.' Kate took a breath to steady herself. 'He's a processor worker. Stands on a cement floor for most of his working day. He complained of tenderness in his right instep.'

'You were thinking of a spur, perhaps?' The blue eye lit enquiringly.

'Certainly a possibility.'

Aiden's mouth went firm for a moment. 'Well, clearly it's not a spur from what we have here. No other bony lesion presenting either.'

'Seems not.' Kate's unwilling gaze followed the stroke of his thumb as it moved rhythmically across his bottom lip in concentration. She whipped her gaze back to the viewing screen and told her heart to settle and her sensible head to reassert itself. 'There are a couple of cysts in the first metatarsal head.' She indicated the shaded outline. 'But they shouldn't present a problem.'

'No.' Aiden O'Connor gave a quick smile, the action cutting interesting grooves into his lean cheeks. 'So, Kate, what treatment will you recommend for your patient?'

Miffed, Kate flicked off the X-ray light. She wasn't aware she'd asked Dr O'Connor to consult with her. Her thoughts began scrambling. And she felt stifled by his nearness, the intimate whisper of peppermint on his breath.

She blinked, then swallowed, flying into professional jargon. 'I'd recommend physio as a priority to try to regain some flexibility.'

'Perhaps a change in the style of his regular work boots or at least some modification could be an option as well. Just suggestions,' he added quickly, interpreting her less-than-impressed look by holding up his hands defensively. 'I won't step on your toes again.'

'You might if we were dancing,' Kate dead-panned. She winced inwardly. Had she really said that?

But O'Connor seemed highly amused. 'Are you inferring I'm a rubbish dancer, Dr Preston?'

'I don't know. Are you?'

'Maybe you'll find out one day,' he answered softly.

Kate wished she could control the odd feeling in her chest when he looked at her. What was it about him? Was it the tantalising stirrings of sexual attraction? The allure of possibility? Whatever it was, it felt different from merely the rush of hormones.

And decidedly uncomfortable.

'We should get this coffee,' she said stiltedly. 'They'll be wondering where we've got to.'

He smiled. 'Let's tell them we got sidetracked.'

Well, that was one explanation for what had just happened here, Kate thought as she stifled the complexity of her feelings and accompanied him along the corridor to the staffroom.

No doubt, she was a looker. Aiden allowed himself a few lazy seconds to observe Kate anew. She was slender, tallish, matching his stride easily. Her eyes were a deep brown, her skin peach perfect. And she was a natural brunette if he was any judge; hair so shiny he could almost see his face in it.

He shook his head as if impatient with his train of thought. He was staring and he'd better stop. He and Kate were colleagues—nothing more.

'Welcome to the zoo,' he said, stretching in front of her to open the door of the staffroom.

Kate's 'Good morning' was met with an answering chorus from the other staff members. Vicki, began pouring coffee into a willow-patterned mug. 'Kate, white with none, right?'

'Thanks, Vic.' Kate smiled. 'But you don't have to wait on me.'

'It's mandatory on your first day,' Aiden quipped.

'What is?' Angelo's dark head came up from the journal he was reading.

'Being nice to Kate on her first day,' Vicki bubbled. 'I brought in a chocolate cake as well.'

'We are blessed.' Angelo's dark eyes behind the silver-framed spectacles glinted with dry humour. 'You'll be brilliant, Kate,' he said, getting to his feet, collecting his journal and moving towards the door. 'Anything you need to consult about, I'm available, as well as Brady and Aiden. Don't hesitate to call on us.'

'Thanks, Angelo. I appreciate that.' Kate took a mouthful of her coffee, feeling it make a warming trail down her throat. They were all being so nice to her.

'Kate, when you have a second, I'll need to clarify one or two points on your personnel file, please?' Monica Lowe, the practice manager, said. 'Nothing urgent.' She smiled, dropping a tea bag into a mug.

'It'll seem odd without Jo.' Natalie Wellings, the practice nurse, said thoughtfully. 'And speaking of your wife, how is she this morning, Brady?'

'Supposedly taking it easy.' Brady's mouth quirked. 'But she said something about rearranging the nursery and colour co-ordinating the baby stuff on the shelves.'

Vicki, who had a one year old tot herself, joked, 'As if that'll last long.'

'Jo's nesting,' Kate came in quietly. 'I remember feeling just like that before both of mine were born…'

Aiden felt something shift inside him as he saw another side of Kate's personality. Suddenly she seemed in her element, her face alight as the baby reminiscences tumbled out. He shrugged inwardly. He didn't have kids. He had nothing to contribute to the conversation. He exited the staffroom quietly.

Kate's day settled into a rhythm, her confidence growing as each patient left, seemingly satisfied with their consultation. And the swarm of butterflies that had been stirring endlessly in her tummy had well and truly settled.

Swinging off her chair, she stretched and prepared to call it a day.

'Oh, Kate?' Vicki tapped and popped her head round the door. 'I've a patient looking really ill. Simone Butler. Could you see her? She said she was due to go on shift at the supermarket but felt so ill she detoured here.' Vicki paused for breath. 'I know you have to pick up your kids soon and I wouldn't ask, but Aiden is on hospital visitation and both Brady and Angelo are on long consults.'

'Ah…' Kate blinked and with the merest glance at her watch, saw her hopes for a reasonably early end to her first day fly out the window. But patients had to come first. 'Of course I'll see her, Vicki. Just give me a minute to call the school and rearrange things for the kids, then show Simone in.'

'I think I've caught flu.' Simone sagged into the chair beside Kate's desk. 'Feel so grotty…'

'Well, if it's flu, there's not much we can do

for you, Simone, except to prescribe the usual rest, paracetamol and fluids.' Kate began a preliminary examination of the young woman. Her temperature was certainly raised and she looked flushed and uncomfortable.

'I took a strong headache tablet at lunchtime,' Simone said as Kate prepared to look down her throat.

'Didn't help?' Kate asked.

'No.'

'Do you get migraines?'

'Never.'

So scrap that theory, Kate thought. 'How about aches and pains in your joints?'

'Mmm. And my back. Feel so sick.' Simone grimaced and scrunched up her eyes. 'Could you close the blinds? Light is killing me...'

In a second, Kate's watchful manner changed to red alert. Her mind reacted like quicksilver, spinning through her patient's symptoms. There were no conclusions but, by heaven, there were some distinct markers.

Meningococcal?

Kate's stomach clenched but her mind stayed clear and calm. There was no room for guessing games here. She needed to act and act quickly. 'Simone, I'm going to give you an injection.'

Checking her patient wasn't allergic, Kate moved with lightning speed across the corridor to the small dispensary. Kate hit the code that would unlock the drugs cabinet and whipped out a prepared dose of penicillin.

She was going by her gut instinct here. That was all she had. But it had never let her down. If Simone had indeed contracted the deadly virus, then vital minutes, even seconds may be all Kate had to save her life. She ran back to her patient.

'I feel c-cold...' Simone's head had dipped forward like a rag doll's.

'Hang in there, honey.' Kate quickly swabbed and plunged the lifesaving drug directly into the vein, knowing full well, they didn't have a proper diagnosis yet. All she could do was buy Simone time. She prayed there was no sign of a rash. But she had to check.

Helping Simone out of her simple shirt-dress

uniform, Kate's examination was meticulous. She knew what she was looking for: a minute scratch mark, a blister, a purple pinprick, any or all of them indicating that bacteria was already present, multiplying by the second in the blood vessels under Simone's skin. If they were there, then Simone's entire body organs were in danger of collapsing.

With relief, Kate saw there was no evidence of a rash. *Yet.* But she wasn't waiting for the possibility.

Instinctively, she began following protocol, snatching up the phone and pressing the key that would connect her with Reception. 'Vicki, would you call an ambulance, please? Tell them we have an emergency hospital admission. And stress the patient is critical.'

'Expect them within a few minutes,' Vicki said. 'I'll run out and open the back doors so they can reverse in.'

'Thanks. Is Natalie about? I could do with some help.'

'She had to leave early,' Vicki sounded dismayed. 'Could I—?'

'No, Vicki. It's fine.' Kate felt put on her mettle. But she'd cope. She needed a space blanket. Diving across the corridor to the treatment room, she searched blindly for a second until she located them. She pulled one from the stockpile and turned to retrace her steps.

'Kate!'

Distracted momentarily from her mission, Kate's head spun towards the voice and saw Aiden striding along the corridor towards her. She slipped back to her consulting room with Aiden on her heels.

'What's up?' He demanded shortly.

'Suspected meningococcal.'

Aiden swore under his breath. 'Ambulance called?'

'On its way.' Kate began tucking the space blanket around her patient.

'What can I do to help?'

'I've done all I can for the moment. But I'll

need to scribble some notes for the admitting MO. Just keep an eye on Simone, if you would.'

'I think she'd be more comfortable if we get her up onto the treatment couch.' So saying, Aiden lifted the young girl as though she weighed no more than an armful of feathers and laid her down gently on her side. She moaned softly.

'Would you recheck for any sign of a rash, please, Aiden?' Kate was scribbling furiously.

'Nothing.' He replaced the space blanket. 'She'll need bloods taken on arrival.'

'All requested.' Kate slashed her signature at the bottom of the notes.

'Ambulance is here, guys.' Vicki appeared at the door.

'Coming through.' A male's deep voice and the squeak of rubber-soled boots echoed along the corridor. Within a very few seconds Simone was loaded onto the trolley.

Kate briefed the paramedic and handed over her notes. 'Thanks for responding so quickly.'

'No worries, Doc. We'll cane it to the hospital now. See you.' The paramedic acknowledged both doctors briefly before heading off.

Kate looked lost for a second. She took a step towards her desk and faltered.

Aiden's hand shot out to her shoulder, heavy and warm. 'Not what you needed on your first day.'

'I'm fine,' Kate said, too quickly. She went to move away but his hand was still on her shoulder and her breath felt fluttery. 'Really.' She firmed her voice. 'I'm fine.'

'Sure?'

'Yes.' She moved from under the weight of his hand. Did he not think of her capable of handling an emergency? 'I'll need to chase up Simone's recent contacts,' she said, thinking aloud. 'Her workplace, home and so on, and check their immunity.' She saw the end of her working day slide further and further away.

'I'll do that.'

'Are you saying I can't do my job?'

Aiden frowned. Why was she so prickly? She looked pressured and he just wanted to help. 'I'm merely suggesting you delegate. I have no patients booked for the rest of the day. Whereas, you're needed elsewhere. You have children to collect from school, don't you?'

Kate dipped her head. She couldn't believe he'd remembered that small detail. And somehow, in ways she couldn't explain, it made her feel vulnerable around him. 'Take some jabs with you in case people's immunity is in question,' she reminded him.

'Kate, I'll handle it.'

Of course he would. She turned away, waiting for her computer to close down. 'I just want Simone safely in isolation and under minute-by-minute observation.'

'And thanks to your quick action, she'll have that.'

'It could still be too late...'

'Don't think like that.' Aiden was firm. But they both knew the effects of the deadly virus. Circulation could fail in the body's extremities—the fingers, toes even whole limbs. Amputations followed. And sometimes death. 'And we don't know for sure it is meningo.'

Kate knew. She'd seen enough cases in her time to be ninety-nine per cent certain. And now she just wanted to collect her kids and hug them to bits. Life was so precious.

Her eyes clouded. It had been an exacting first day and if she being honest she did feel drained, both physically and mentally, but that would pass as things both at work and home began settling into a rhythm…

What the hell was she still hanging around for? Aiden's mouth compressed briefly. She seemed lost in thought, miles away. 'Kate, there's no more you can do here,' he said. 'Your children must be waiting for you.'

Kate pushed up from her desk. 'They're being well taken care of.'

Watching her face, Aiden saw her bottom lip pull into a tight little moue. What now? Did she think he was criticising her parenting? A muscle worked in his jaw. She'd wrong-footed him again. And he didn't like the feeling one little bit.

Kate blinked uncertainly. Why was O'Connor staring at her like that—as if she'd grown an extra nose or something? She'd handed over to him and he should be gone. 'Vicki will have Simone's details.'

'I'm on it. And I'll brief Angelo and Brady. Want me to give you a call later and report my findings?'

'If you wouldn't mind.' The doctors exchanged mobile numbers as a matter of course.

'Why would I mind?' He shrugged, the movement of his shoulders drawing attention to the interplay of muscles under his close-fitting shirt.

Kate looked down quickly, searching the bottom of her handbag for her keys. Locating them, she hitched up her medical case. 'Thanks for your help.'

'Yep.' Their eyes met and he could see the wariness, the uncertain flicker in her gaze. He moved to the door with her. 'Drive carefully.'

She gave him a taut smile. 'Kids in the car. Always do'

Watching her departure, Aiden felt as though

an invisible punch had landed in his solar plexus, robbing him not just of oxygen but of plain common sense as well. His gaze stayed riveted on the sassy swing of her hips, her slender waist, the toss of her dark head as she pulled open the outer door to the car park.

Yanking his eyes off her neat little backside, he pushed back the zing in his bloodstream. Have you entirely lost your marbles, O'Connor? he asked himself. He shook his head as if to clear it. He had far more urgent things to do than to stand ogling Kate Preston.

CHAPTER TWO

KATE stabbed the key into the ignition. The ebb and flow of her first day swirled around her. For a second she leaned her head back against the seat and took stock. She thought she'd fitted in successfully with the practice partners—except for Aiden. Why did she seem to be having these little run-ins with him? She prided herself on the fact she wasn't difficult to work with. But with him she felt continuously put on her mettle. Off balance.

Well, she had no time to analyse it now. In a defiant little twist, she started the engine and eased out of her parking space. She couldn't wait to see her kids.

The school provided care for the students both before and after school. And nowadays, with most families juggling work and family commitments, the facility had become a necessity.

Kate had been well pleased with the set-up and the supervising staff had seemed both pleasant and clued in to the needs of the children. Luke and Mia would be safe and well looked after and that was all she could hope for.

'Mummy! Mummy!' Mia ran across the room and threw herself against her mother's legs.

Kate bent to her small daughter's level and hugged her tightly. Then she leaned back and cupped Mia's chin. 'Did you have a good day at school, baby?'

Mia's little shrug went almost to her ears. ''S OK. I looked and looked for you after school.'

Kate felt a lump in her throat and a pang of sadness that circumstances wouldn't allow her to be a full-time mother. It would have been wonderful, at least until Mia was a little older. 'I had to stay later at work. Didn't your teacher explain?'

The little one nodded slowly. 'But I still looked and looked.'

Of course she had. Young things always looked for their mothers. Kate uncurled upright, keeping Mia closely at her side. 'Shall we find Lukie now? Then we'll all be able to go home.'

Home was a pleasant cottage Kate was leasing. On the whole, it was serving their needs, at least for the present. After high-rise apartment living in Sydney, she'd yearned for a sense of peace, that had alluded her since she'd become a widow and returned from the United States. Peace, light and the outdoors, she affirmed now as she eased her car into the garage at the side of the house.

Ten minutes later, Kate had shucked off the trappings of her professional life, showered and pulled on baggy shorts and T-shirt. Gathering up the children, she went next door to her neighbours', Patrick and Eileen Kelly. The Kellys were friends of her parents and it was they who had let Kate know of the cottage's availability.

'Do we have to?' Luke moaned, as they made their way along the path at the side of the Kelly's house towards the back garden.

'Yes, we do,' Kate said calmly, ignoring her son's stubborn, determined look. 'You have to say sorry to Mr Kelly for almost maiming one of his chickens with your soccer ball.'

'Those bantams are stupid,' Luke maintained with childish candour.

'Not to Mr Kelly.' Kate realised she could have let the incident pass. Patrick and Eileen were grandparents themselves. They knew about little boys and footballs. But even at eight Luke was capable of learning about being responsible for his actions.

Kate stifled the recurring thoughts of the long road ahead as a sole parent. Everything, every decision was going to be down to her. She'd have to be disciplinarian, counsellor, role model but mostly, and more importantly, she needed always to be a loving mum.

Patrick and Eileen were sitting on their outdoor chairs under a shady tree. 'Hello, you three.' Eileen smiled at Kate and the children, raising a plump hand in greeting. 'All done for the day?'

'Here, sit down, love.' Patrick got to his feet

and beckoned Kate across the lawn. 'I'm about to feed the bantams. You kids like to help?' He looked keenly at Luke and Mia.

There was a bit of psychology going on here, Kate thought, and thanked heaven for Patrick's insight. 'Go on,' she urged with a smile when Luke looked hesitant. 'It's good to learn new things.'

'Is the bantam I hit with my ball OK?'

Kate heard Luke's version of an apology as the trio made their way to the far end of the yard and the hen coop. 'Thanks, Eileen,' Kate said on a breathy sigh of relief.

The older woman looked perplexed. 'For what, dear?'

Kate lifted a shoulder. 'For being so understanding about the football. It was careless of Luke. It could so easily have been a window.'

'Or someone's head,' Eileen cackled. 'Kids will be kids, Kate. And there was no real harm done. Patrick and I were just saying what a grand job you're doing, raising your two.'

A little half-smile flickered on Kate's mouth.

She didn't want to admit to Eileen that sometimes the *job* felt almost crippling. But she had to look forward with hope. Nothing else would do. She regrouped quickly and got to her feet. 'You know, I think I'll go and join Patrick and the kids.' She forced herself to sound bright and chirpy. 'It's years since I fed the chickens.'

Kate quickly caught up with the little group.

'Luke says bantams are stupid.'

Kate cringed inside at her daughter's bald statement. Kids had no idea of diplomacy.

Patrick seemed unconcerned. He turned his weathered face and sent Kate a wry half-smile before turning his attention back to Luke. 'You know, young fella, a lot of folk think that about bantams. Reckon they're silly and noisy. But my girls are just happy to scratch around and lay beautiful little eggs.'

'So, they're like *real* chickens?' Luke showed a modicum of interest in the small black feathery birds.

'Oh, yes.' Patrick nodded wisely. 'And now they're about ready to turn in for the night.' He moved towards the feed bin, allocating the children a small container each. With a flick of his hand, he showed them how to scatter the grain.

The bantams gobbled up the food and then one by one, in strict pecking order, began to wander off to their roost.

'They have such tiny feet,' Mia said in wonderment. 'And they go to bed very early.'

Patrick smiled down at the beguiling little girl. 'They get up very early as well. In the summertime, as early as four o'clock in the morning.' Still smiling, he ushered the children from the chicken coop and closed the gate.

'And we'd better get home too.' Kate walked between the children, her hands resting on their small shoulders. 'Thanks, Patrick,' she added softly.

Several minutes later they were back at their front gate, the children each carefully carrying a perfect little brown egg for their tea.

Friday afternoon.

In an end-of-working-day gesture, Kate raised

her arms and stretched. It had been a busy week and she was tired, yet at the same time exhilarated. She was holding her own. That thought gave her immense satisfaction.

In weekend mode, she got to her feet, collected her things and made her along the corridor to the doctors' weekly staff meeting.

She was the last to arrive. Only four chairs had been placed at the table for the meeting. And the only one vacant was next to Aiden. A dozen disturbing thoughts collided in Kate's head. Oh, for heaven's sake. He was just a man, wasn't he? And if there was chemistry, so what? So nothing. She took her place beside Aiden, vividly conscious of his body warmth, the faint drift of apple laundry softener on his shirt.

Aiden turned his head and smiled at her 'Water?'

'Sounds good.' Kate smiled back at him and then wished she hadn't. There was such an easiness about him, an almost arrogant sexiness that was a threat to her sensibilities.

'Thanks.' She took a sip from the glass and then placed it in front of her.

'Right.' Angelo settled his glasses more comfortably and looked expectantly around at his colleagues. 'Who wants to be first cab off the rank? Kate, your patient with meningo? What's her prognosis?'

'So far she's holding her own.' Kate looked around at the practice team. 'But it will be a long haul for her. And her family. They've only moved here recently to new jobs. Now their whole lives have been thrown into chaos.'

'On the other hand,' Angelo came in quietly, 'they should be very thankful for your swift diagnosis. Community medicine at its best, Kate. Well done.'

'Hear, hear,' Brady and Aiden concurred.

'Thanks.' Kate felt a lift in her spirits, warmed by her colleagues' approval. 'We had an outbreak of meningococcal when I was working in the States,' she offloaded modestly. 'The symptoms are something you don't forget in a hurry.'

'I don't know if I'd have jumped on it so

quickly,' Brady admitted candidly. 'It's been a long time since I saw a case.'

Aiden leaned back in his chair, tapping his pen end to end on the table. 'Well, it's always better to err on the side of caution and give the antibiotics anyway, as Kate did.'

'I'm sure we're all agreed on that.' Angelo shuffled his notes into a neat pile.

The meeting eventually wound to a close.

'OK, guys, if no one has any further business, that's it.' Angelo tucked his pen into his shirt pocket. 'Kate, your caseload manageable?'

Before Kate could answer, Aiden said, 'I think we should make sure Kate's patient list for the afternoon surgery doesn't run over.'

Kate's chin came up, disbelief widening her gaze. Dammit. What on earth did O'Connor think he was doing? She didn't need him advocating for her. She could fight her own corner. 'That happened only on Monday,' she pointed out thinly. 'And the circumstances were extraordinary.'

Aiden blinked. Her angry little thrust as she turned towards him revealed the creamy skin of her throat and upper chest. He felt his body grow hot, imagining the tip of his tongue traversing that same silky skin. He blinked the thought away as if it had the power to rear up and bite him. 'I just think your special needs should take priority.'

Special needs? Kate pursed her lips disapprovingly. Where did he get off making a loaded comment like that? He'd made her sound like some kind of basket case.

'I'm sure Kate will speak up if she needs any change in her surgery hours,' Brady came in smoothly. 'Right, Kate?'

Kate sent him a grateful nod, temporarily unable to find words.

'Good, good.' Always the mediator, Angelo was brisk, gathering up his notes. 'I'm on call at the after-hours clinic over the weekend. What about the rest of you—Brady, any plans?'

'Nah.' Brady leaned back in his chair, his fingers drumming a lazy tattoo on the tabletop. 'Staying close to home.'

Aiden chuckled. 'Figures.' He arched back, raising his arms in a long stretch. 'What about you, Kate? What kind of weekend do you have planned?'

As if he cared. And it was none of his business anyway. Kate felt like poking her tongue at him. But that would have been totally juvenile. She jerked a shoulder in a careless shrug. 'Cleaning the house and doing the laundry will be high on my agenda.'

'Riveting stuff, then,' he said.

She shot him a look, certain she hadn't imagined the trace of boredom in his tone. Well, nice for some. He didn't have kids to consider when he made his weekend plans. 'What about you, then, Dr O'Connor?' she asked. Not that she cared.

'I'm going sky-diving. Should be a good day for it.'

Kate's insides froze. A good day for what—killing himself? She felt sick to the stomach, drowned in a thousand memories. Scooping up her notes, she got to her feet. 'Um—excuse me. I have to collect my children.' Suddenly she needed to fill her lungs with good, clean air.

Frowning, Aiden watched her almost run from the room. He gave a short humourless laugh and shot a wordless query at his male colleagues.

'Kate's husband was killed in a sky-diving accident,' Brady supplied gruffly.

'Oh, God…' Aiden's breath of disbelief hitched to a halt. 'Why did no one tell me?' He shot a pained look at the two men.

'Kate and I had a quiet chat after her appointment had been confirmed,' Angelo looked contrite. 'She told me then.'

'And I found out from Jo,' Brady said. 'She and Kate have become friends.' He looked at Aiden and gave an apologetic open-handed shrug. 'Sorry, mate. I thought you would have known.'

Saturday.

How long was a fair time to grieve? Kate wondered as she placed the last of the breakfast dishes in the drainer. It had been three years and surely now it was time to stop. A stray sunbeam burst through the open window, catching the fine gold of her wedding ring.

Was that a sign? she wondered. Perhaps, to be fully free so she could move forward, the ring had to go.

Her breath almost stilled as she eased the wedding band from her finger. Happy-go-lucky Cory. She'd loved him with all her heart. She couldn't imagine falling in love again, let alone going to bed with someone other than Cory. She cast the rather desolate thought away. Hadn't she just convinced herself it was time to move on?

Being outdoors seemed like a plan, she thought, going out onto the deck that overlooked the back garden. The kids were happily engaged. Luke was bouncing his soccer ball off the brick wall that separated the garage from the garden, while Mia had staked out a strip of the concrete path and was playing a game of hopscotch.

Well, she'd take a leaf out of her children's book, Kate thought. She'd get cracking on the garden. She had some daisies she wanted to thin out and replant and there was bound to be some weeding that needed doing.

Ignoring the thump, thump of Luke's ball, Kate got to work with her trowel. The smell in the air was simply glorious, she mused as she hacked her way through the clumps of daisies. A sweet pungency drifted up from the earth and while Kate worked, two leaves of gold and brown fluttered down beside her. Finally, she was done, stripping off her gloves and flexing her fingers thankfully.

But there was still one more job she had to do. The lower hinge on the lattice gate of the little fern house was hanging by a thread.

Exhaling a small sigh of resignation, she inspected her meagre supply of tools, finally selecting a screwdriver that might do the job. Squatting beside the gate, she began to work on replacing the screw. 'Oh, blast!' she muttered as the recalcitrant bit of metal fell sideways onto the grass.

'What are you trying to do?'

Kate felt a ripple along her spine, like a bird sensing a predator. She'd have known that voice anywhere. She didn't look up. 'What brings you by, Aiden?'

'Just passing. Thought I'd call in.'

And if she believed that, she'd believe there was a practical use for chocolate teapots.

'Here give it to me,' he said, hunkering down beside her and holding out a long-fingered hand.

Kate gritted her teeth, slapping the screw-driver into his palm like a surgical instrument. She jerked upright, her eyes fixed on his broad shoulders under the black T-shirt as they flexed to give his arms more impetus, putting the final twist on the large metal screw.

'General maintenance should be part of your lease,' Aiden said, uncoiling upwards beside her. 'Where's your landlord?'

Kate huffed a derogatory laugh. 'Out of the country mostly.'

'Bummer.'

He chuckled softly and Kate felt as though she'd been dipped in a vat of warm, rich chocolate. Her heart did a few skips and she looked away hastily. 'I thought you were going sky-diving'.

'That was at five o'clock this morning,' he dismissed. 'I've been up for ages.' A beat of silence. 'Are *you* OK?'

She looked at him then, caught by the sincerity of his tone. 'Why wouldn't I be?'

His blue eyes hazed for a moment. 'Yesterday… after the meeting. You were upset. My fault, I think. My remarks were thoughtless.' He gave a self-deprecating half-smile. 'Anyway…my sincere apologies.'

'It's fine. Don't worry about it. You weren't to know. Perhaps I overreacted anyway.' Agitatedly, she lifted a hand and scooped a strand of hair away from her shirt collar.

'I don't want things to be awkward between us, Kate.'

'They won't be,' she affirmed quickly.

Aiden felt a weird tightening in his chest. So far, so good but now there seemed nowhere for the conversation to go. That was until the children, curious about their mother's visitor, nudged in beside her.

Kate gathered them in, her smiling mouth soft and pretty. 'Aiden, these are my children, Luke and Mia. Kids, this is Dr O'Connor from the surgery.'

'Luke. Mia.' O'Connor greeted them almost formally. 'I'm Aiden.'

'Can you play soccer?' Luke asked hopefully.

'You bet I can. Can you?'

'A bit. But there's no room to practise here.' Luke looked dolefully around the back garden.

'Ah…' Aiden rubbed his chin thoughtfully. He turned to Kate. 'There's a great park near the showgrounds. Have you not found it yet?'

'There's hardly been time. Perhaps we could go across later.' She tried to placate Luke with the promise.

'I could take him for a kick-about now,' Aiden said before he knew he was going to say it.

'Thanks, but I can't let you do that,' Kate protested quietly. She made a small face. Oh, lord, this was awkward.

'Of course. I understand.' Aiden spread his hands in mute acceptance. 'You hardly know me after all.'

It wasn't just that. Kate battled with conflicting emotions. Was it wise to allow Aiden to become involved in their lives so quickly? Or at all, for that matter? But on the other hand, it would be so good for Luke to have some male company. Her dad did his best but now in his late-sixties, understandably, his energy levels were flagging. And Aiden was young. *More like a real dad.*

Kate felt discomfort flood her. Too far. Too fast. She dithered a second too long.

'Can I, Mum?' Luke piped up, his tone wheedling, his big brown eyes pleading.

'Why don't we *all* go to the park?' Aiden suggested, forcing himself not to reach out, not to touch Kate. He wanted to reassure her that he, Aiden O'Connor, was trustworthy. He wanted to see her relax, make her laugh.

Stop her acting so uptight around him. He wanted to get to know her a whole lot better. A whole lot. And away from from the constraints of the surgery.

'All of us?' Kate said, and frowned a bit.

'Seems sensible.'

Kate's heart twitched and kept on twitching while Aiden's smile warmed, deepened, drawing her in. 'OK, then.' She flapped her hands in an airy motion of acceptance. 'I'll put together a few snacks and things. We may as well make a morning of it.'

Mia jigged in excitement. 'Are there any swings?' she asked Aiden.

'And monkey bars.'

Kate felt her heart turn over, watching Aiden hunker down beside her daughter, diminishing the impact of his height. 'And rope ladders,' he told Mia seriously. 'Even a flying fox.'

'She's too little for that,' Luke chimed in importantly.

'Am not.' Mia's fierce little look told him what she thought of that.

'Perhaps if I hold onto Mia, she could manage the flying fox.' Aiden pursed his lips as if considering the problem. 'What do you think, Luke?'

'Yeah, I s'pose.' Luke gave grudging approval.

Good grief, he was a natural. Kate ran up the steps to the deck. Her heart felt as though it might burst. They looked so right together, Aiden O'Connor and her kids. She shouldn't think it, but she did.

Kate couldn't believe how fast the morning had flown. True to his promise, Aiden had put Luke through his paces. He'd been patient, encouraging and Luke had responded, his little face lit with happiness as Aiden showed him how to kick with the side of his boot and not the toe, as Luke had been doing. The results had been spectacular. Well, at least to his mother.

Kate thanked Aiden again as they took a breather. They were sitting on the wooden bench seat, their backs resting against the picnic table while the children played nearby. 'This has been absolutely wonderful for Luke,' Kate said. 'I wouldn't have had a clue about any of that technique stuff.'

'Horses for courses, Kate.' Aiden took a bite from the apple she'd tossed to him. 'I coach for the local juniors. Would you consider allowing Luke to join one of our teams?'

Kate took her time answering. 'I guess it would be good for him.'

'I wouldn't be coaching his age group,' Aiden said casually. 'I coach A level.'

'Oh.'

'But all the coaches are accredited. Luke would be in good hands. He'd have fun with his peers. And at his young age, playing sport should be about having fun. Don't you agree?'

Aiden watched her thoughtful reaction to the concept. She tilted her face towards him, her hair brushing against his shoulder, a mess of windblown waves, long, shiny and smelling of citrus. Fabulous. He breathed in deeply to stop himself leaning into her and closing the space between them. Touching his mouth to hers.

But one touch would never be enough.

Kate tilted her chin. Aiden O'Connor had given up a whole morning to spend time with her children and yet he hadn't seemed bored or indifferent. Well, if he was, he hadn't let it show. In fact, he'd been unassuming and *nice.* And now he was smiling at her, his mouth tilting quizzically. He seemed in no hurry to leave, his tanned legs in their cargo shorts stretched out in front of him, his trainer-clad feet crossed at the ankles.

Avoiding his gaze, Kate dipped her head, locking her fingers around the edge of the bench seat. What was the question again? Oh, yes, *having fun.* There hadn't been much fun in her own life recently but her kids deserved a truckload. She swallowed hard and then said huskily, 'Childhood should all be about fun.'

'I'll let you know when sign-on day is happening, then, and you can bring Luke along.' Aiden glanced at his watch. 'And talking about fun, I should make tracks. Party in Brisbane tonight I can't possibly miss.'

'I won't hold you up, then.' Kate rocked to

her feet. She felt sick with embarrassment. For just a little while she'd allowed herself to relax around Aiden O'Connor, to edge closer to him, mentally as well as physically. But he obviously had personal ties she knew nothing about. And it was none of her business anyway.

Aiden got to his feet slowly. What had he said? She'd already bolted, rounding up Luke and Mia as if she couldn't wait to be shot of him.

'Say, thank you to Dr O'Connor, kids.' Kate tightened all the bits of herself that had seemed to have loosened, almost presenting the children to him for inspection. She felt such a fool. Letting herself be lulled by the sheer sexiness of the man. Letting herself begin to want things…

'Kate.' Aiden dismissed the children's thanks gently. 'What's wrong?'

Kate's heart flipped and her throat went dry. 'What makes you think something's wrong?'

'Your body language for starters.'

A soft breeze had whipped up, almost adding to the tension. Aiden watched as a tendril of hair flickered across Kate's cheek and hung.

On a reflex action he reached out and pleated it back. Her hair was as soft as he'd imagined. Silken. 'Going to tell me?'

His blue eyes glinted, demanding an answer.

Kate's heart hammered, her lips parted, her brown eyes burned like simmering coals. She wanted to reach up and place her hand against his. Increase the pressure against her skin. *Connect* with him. But that was madness. And it was as if a sign came up in front of her saying, *No through road.* 'You're imagining things.' Her voice was barely there.

'You know I'm not.' Aiden pressed his shoes into the ground, anchoring himself. His throat convulsed in a dry deep swallow. 'Kate…'

'Just leave it, Aiden.' She ducked away out of reach and shepherded the children towards the car.

Frowning, Aiden picked up the picnic basket and followed.

Luke and Mia had already scrambled into the rear seat and buckled their seat belts. Kate held the boot open, waiting for him. 'Thanks,' she said gruffly, almost slamming the lid on his fingers. 'See you at work on Monday.'

She fled before he could answer, throwing herself into the driver's seat, and was away within seconds, while his thought processes drew to a screaming halt. His mouth twisted into a grim line. What was with her?

Oh, hell. Shaking his head at the complexities of it all, he wandered across to his off-road vehicle. Would he ever get it right around Kate Preston?

CHAPTER THREE

KATE kept herself busy for the rest of the day, the events of the morning running over in her mind. Aiden O'Connor obviously had a *life.* A life Kate knew nothing about. And yet… Kate shook her head. Surely she hadn't imagined the sense of intimacy she'd experienced between them that morning? Perhaps he just liked women running after him, she thought sourly. The thrill of the chase.

Did she want to be part of that chase? Out of nowhere, she relived the feeling of the weight of his hand against her skin. Imagined her body awakening to his all-over touch. Oh, get real, Kate, she implored inwardly. Hefting the laundry basket onto her hip, she went through to the bedroom and began sorting the clean clothes into neat piles.

But however hard she tried, at the end of the day she still felt at sixes and sevens, as though a huge boulder had been thrown into the pool of uniformity that was currently her life.

It was something of a relief when Jo McNeal phoned on Sunday morning. 'Hi, Kate. Do you have plans today?'

'Nothing more interesting than the ironing. What's up?'

'What about coming out to our place for lunch? Brady's barbecuing.'

'Oh, that sounds nice.' Kate's spirits lifted. The McNeals lived on acreage out of town a bit.

'So, you'll come?'

'Love to. Is it OK for Luke to bring his wretched football?

Jo chuckled. 'Driving you nuts, is he?'

'Just a bit.'

'Then get on out here,' Jo insisted. 'We've loads of space. Luke can go wild. Now, what about finding us? Are you clued in?'

'Ish…'

Jo chuckled. 'Grab a pen, then, and I'll give you explicit directions.'

'This is all so lovely,' Kate said. With the children off playing happily under Brady's watchful eye, Jo was showing her over the gardens surrounding the old farmhouse they had renovated.

'It is, isn't it?' Jo said proudly. 'The house was built in the 1840s. I'm still discovering beautiful old roses that have survived in the oddest places. And when Brady stripped back years of undergrowth, we found grapevines still viable.'

Kate's look was wistful as she gazed past the rustic bench seat to the gently sloping paddocks and further on to the mountains, misty blue and beautiful. 'So it's all been a fabulous adventure, then?'

'If you discount the odd snake or two,' Jo said wryly. 'But we've got the house just about right so that's a relief with the new baby coming.' She touched Kate's arm. 'Enough of the tour for now. Let's go indoors and get a cuppa before the company arrives.'

'Oh.' Kate sent a pained look down at her T-shirt and jeans.

'Just family.' Jo smiled. 'Brady's parents are coming out from Brisbane. They're spending a couple of days with us.'

Kate hooked an eyebrow. 'More doctors?'

'Blessedly, no.' Jo gave a curl of laughter. 'Vivienne is a barrister, James is head of town planning with the city council. They're lovely. Been so good to us. They're terrific grandparents to Andrew and will be to this little one as well.' Jo touched her bump protectively. 'I guess we're about to become one of those *blended* families,' she added philosophically.

'Has it been difficult?' Kate got mugs down from the dresser.

'Not so far because I've been in Andrew's life since he was a baby but perhaps when he's older and has questions about his birth mother…' Jo stopped and shrugged a shoulder.

Kate looked thoughtful. Not for the first time she wondered how Luke and Mia would feel about a stepfather—that's if she ever found anyone who actually wanted the role. It would be a huge decision to allow a new man into their lives. But their memories of Cory were a bit sketchy now, especially Mia's.

'Why the big sigh?' Kate slid home-made gingerbread onto a plate.

'Oh—nothing.' Kate gave an embarrassed laugh.

'Thinking about blended families?'

Jo's direct look left no room for Kate to waffle. She said slowly, 'Luke and Mia are eight and six. I sometimes wonder…that is, if I did meet someone…'

Jo poured the tea. 'Kate, if he loved you, he'd love your children. Stands to reason, doesn't it? *Have* you met someone?' she asked perceptively.

'In Mt Pryde?'

'Hey.' Jo wagged a finger. 'Don't write off the possibility. It happened for Brady and me.' Jo gave a believe-it-or-not wide-eyed look. 'And for a very good friend of mine, Fliss O'Byrne. She came to work at the local hospital and, wham, fell head over heels for the medical director, Callum. They're blissfully happy.'

Kate suddenly felt uneasy. The last thing she needed was for Jo to start matchmaking. Even if it was well intentioned. She drummed up a passable smile. 'I'll be sure to keep an open mind, then.'

They talked generalities then until Jo exclaimed, 'Look at the time! The grandparents'll be here any minute. I'd better give Brady a shout and start setting up for lunch. I'll think we'll eat out on the verandah. It's such a lovely day.'

'Jo, let me help.' Kate got to her feet. 'What would you like me to do?'

'Well, I thought we'd feed the kids first. Then we can relax over a drink and eat a bit later, if that's OK with you?'

'Perfectly. It'll be bliss just to have someone else cook.' Kate loaded a tray with table mats, plates and cutlery. 'So, I'll set for five adults, then?'

'Mmm, looks that way. I tried to call Aiden earlier. His place is just a few ks further on from here. Thought he might have liked to join us for lunch. He does sometimes. My call went through to his voice mail. He's probably away somewhere for the weekend.'

Kate kept her gaze locked firmly on the tray in her hands. She knew exactly where Aiden was.

On his way back from Brisbane that Sunday afternoon, Aiden's thoughts were on Kate. He hadn't yet decided what to do about her. Yet he knew there was *something* going on between them. And Kate knew as well.

He prided himself on relating to women. But with Kate it was like trying to unravel a complex work of art. It made him feel restless, even groping a bit for the right approach. He didn't want her feeling ill at ease around him. Suddenly and for reasons he couldn't explain he felt right out of his comfort zone.

Flicking on the radio, he listened to the last of a sports broadcast, snorted at the final result and flicked it off again. Slackening his speed, he drove through the town centre and then picked up speed again as he headed for home.

Usually he felt a surge in his spirits as he took the rural scenic road to his property, Three Oaks. Today he felt restless, hardly noticing the colourful patchwork of cultivated crops on either side of the road. The multitude of lush colours and textures of the vegetation might have been a dull grey for all he noticed.

The white wooden gates of the McNeals' place were coming up. Aiden thought for a second, then slowed and turned in. Jo was a sweetheart. She'd be sure to have the kettle on and he could murder a strong black coffee. And some uncomplicated company.

Jo had seen Aiden arrive and went out on to the verandah to greet him.

'Sorry I missed your call.' He leaned sideways and buzzed her cheek. 'Any coffee going?'

'As always.' Jo chuckled and led the way along to the kitchen. 'You've just missed Kate.'

Aiden feigned scant interest, better than trying to analyse his odd reaction at just hearing her name. 'Kate Preston?'

Jo rolled her eyes. 'Do we know another Kate?' Jo slipped an expresso coffee bag into a mug. 'I invited her and the kids for lunch. It's got to be a bit lonely for her here at the moment. Don't you think?'

'Maybe. I hadn't thought about it.' *Liar.* 'Where are Andrew and Brady?' He changed tack swiftly and dropped on to a high kitchen stool.

Jo wasn't fooled for a second. She'd seen the smear of colour redden his throat at the mention of Kate's name. So that's the way the land lay. Interesting. She handed Aiden his coffee. 'Andrew wore himself out playing with Kate's two and is having a nap. Brady's folks are visiting. They've all gone for a bit of a wander down to the creek.'

Aiden nodded. 'Coffee's good, thanks.'

'Nice weekend?' Jo asked lightly.

'On the whole, yes.' And it has been, he thought, if you discounted the hash he'd made of things on Saturday morning. Oh, God, he was back to that and didn't want to be. He finished his coffee, swung off his stool and rinsed his mug at the sink.

Kate was full of misgivings as she drove to work on Monday. Somehow she had to establish a manageable working relationship with Aiden. But would he respond?

She'd given herself a talking-to last night. She'd entirely overreacted on Saturday morning. When she should have acted cool and light, she'd been tense and awkward around him. I'm so out of practice, she wailed silently. God, I've been such heavy going!

In the staffroom, Kate sipped at a coffee she didn't want and tried to join in the pre-work chatter. There was no sign of Aiden and every time the door opened her nerves shredded a little more. Yet he had to be here somewhere. She'd seen his Land Rover in the car park.

When Vicky headed off about her business, Kate seized her chance and exited discreetly after her. She caught up with Vicky in Reception. 'Oh, Vic, is Aiden in? I need to check something with him.'

'In his room.' Vicky went through the hatch and began switching on computers and fax machine. 'Catching up on paperwork apparently.'

Kate nodded, feeling the twist of nerves in her stomach. 'How's my list looking?' she sidetracked quickly.

'You're booked wall to wall, Kate. Breanna Cassen is your first patient. Remember, we spoke about her on Friday when we were juggling appointments—mum with the poorly baby?'

'Yes.' Kate turned to leave. 'I'll bring myself up to date before she comes in. Thanks, Vic.' Kate went directly to Aiden's consulting room.

Standing outside his door, she took a deep, controlling breath, her heart a drumbeat in her chest. She lifted her hand and knocked. Hearing his gruff 'Yes?' she pushed open the door and went in.

'Morning.' She forced a tentative smile. 'Do you have a minute?'

'Kate.' Aiden looked surprised. Even startled. Kate watched as he quickly schooled his expression. He'd obviously been miles away, broodingly intent on something…or someone.

'Have a seat,' he offered, scooting his own chair back from the desk to a more informal setting.

'I won't, thanks. I just wanted to say…' Kate licked her lips. 'I realise we seem to have…'

Aiden couldn't bear her discomfort. Swinging up from his chair, he leaned towards her, his hands planted firmly on the desk between them. 'Kate, it's OK.'

'No, it's not. I need to say this. I've been acting like a lunatic, feeling awkward…'

'Around me?'

'Yes… I guess.' She felt the shallow tightness in her breathing, her voice petering away to nothing. She should say what she'd come to say and get out but something in his look, his manner held her motionless.

'I see.' Aiden's eyes were like blue chips. He wasn't letting her run from this. This awareness was mutual, whatever spin she chose to put on it. 'What do you suggest we do about it, then?'

Kate sent him a beseeching look. Suddenly his office seemed too small, too intimate. She looked around jerkily for inspiration. 'I'm not usually difficult to work with…'

'Neither am I.' Quite deliberately he moved around the corner of his desk, closer to her. 'So we agree we don't actually dislike each other, then?'

Far from it. Kate looked at him wordlessly. This was not how any of it was supposed to happen. Her heart tripped. 'Aiden, I…'

'Yes, Kate?' He could see her chest rising and falling more quickly, hear the plaintive little catch in her breathing. And he'd never been more turned on in his life.

He moved closer, put out his hands and closed on her upper arms.

At his touch, Kate felt the sudden wild dip in her stomach, the violent beating of her heart. She tried to swallow but it was difficult, raspy. 'I just need some space…'

'You don't.' Aiden applied pressure through his hands, capturing her in one easy movement, aligning her body with his. 'You don't need space, Kate. This is what you need. What we both need—isn't it?'

Kate felt her legs turn to jelly, her safe world implode, as his mouth descended on hers swiftly, cutting off any response she might have made.

Aiden felt her lips, soft and giving, his for the taking, and he plundered them in a brief, hard kiss. 'You still want space?' he said huskily, breaking away with what little willpower he had left.

Kate sensed her safe world tipping crazily. She felt dazed and reeling from the passionate storm. His lips had sought a long overdue awakening and she felt the essence of it tugging at the very core of her femininity.

'Aiden—'

He claimed her mouth again, this time more slowly, but still passionate, greedy, demanding entry, stoking the heat to a wildfire. He felt the moment she finally acknowledged her truth, her weight pressing against him, her arms tightening around his neck. In an action that was pure reflex, pure male, he dropped his hands from her shoulders to encircle her backside.

Kate felt a shudder go through her. She felt hot, desire rocking her like an earthquake.

And she wanted to feel. *Feel.* It had been so long since she'd done this. And there were no thoughts of tomorrow, of kids, her job. Aiden's kisses were like sweet, dark wine. And she wanted to drink every last drop.

'Kate…' Aiden dragged his mouth away, his breath coming in harsh gulps. 'Not here.'

She blinked uncomprehendingly. 'Oh.' She put a hand to her still-tingling mouth and shot him an agonised look.

'Don't.' Aiden drew a shaky breath. His body was still aroused, every nerve in his groin on fire. He reached out to touch her, dropping his hand when she flinched back. 'Don't start regretting this, Kate,' he warned softly.

Kate shook her head. How had she let this happen? And to let it happen here in their workplace—that was unpardonable. She felt her face flame. 'We have patients.' She whirled, almost tripping in her haste, and fled.

Instead of turning towards her office, Kate instinctively bolted to the bathroom at the other end of the corridor. She fell against the wash basin, setting the tap running and splashing cold water on her face over and over. Finally she closed off the tap and straightened, regarding herself in the mirror above the basin, her intake of breath almost audible. She shook her head in disbelief. This was someone she didn't know. Calm and professional Dr Kate Preston was nowhere to be seen. Instead, there was an imposter. A woman with wild eyes, passion-flushed cheeks and a mouth that looked…soft, with the lush ripeness of the darkest plum.

What on earth am I doing? she silently asked the reflection. What on earth have I *done*?

Aiden felt like throwing things. What on earth had he done? He'd crossed the line. That's what he'd done. He swore under his breath, ramming the heels of his hands against his eyes. Big black mark, O'Connor. Where in God's name had his self-control been?

Back at her desk, Kate fought for composure, her conscience battling with her libido. She had to blank Aiden out. Had to. She straightened in her chair to quell the ache deep inside her.

Directing her attention towards Breanna Cassen's history gave her the hiatus she needed to compose her thoughts. She noted that the young mum had had her early prenatal care with Jo McNeal and then the family had moved to Brisbane where Breanna's baby boy, Thomas, had been born with congenital torticollis. Kate knew the term usually meant a twisted neck. She'd encountered several cases when she'd worked in the States. Now it seemed the Cassen family had returned to Mt Pryde and had automatically gone onto Kate's list.

When Breanna arrived, Kate ushered her in.

'You're new, aren't you?' Breanna said, dropping into a chair and setting Thomas in his carry capsule beside her on the floor.

'Yes, I'm new to the practice.' Kate gave a contained little smile. 'I've taken over Dr McNeal's patients. How can I help you today, Breanna?'

'It's Thomas.' The young mother's face worked for a second. 'I'm worried sick about him.' She turned pleading eyes to Kate. 'Will he ever be normal?'

'Has it been explained to you just what torticollis is?' Kate fielded the question skilfully.

'The paediatrician at the hospital said something about his neck muscles being pulled when he was born.'

'Sometimes because of trauma,' Kate said. 'There is a tiny tear in the muscle fibres and this in turn leads to bruising and scar tissue forming. I understand you've had Thomas to a physiotherapist?'

Breanna nodded. 'A couple of weeks ago. We have to do exercises with him every day. But there doesn't seem any improvement.'

'It's early days.' Kate tone was reassuring.

'The stretching exercises you would have been shown are designed to extend the tight muscle and relieve the tension in it. Sometimes it takes two or three months to see an improvement.'

Breanna's thin shoulders rose and fell as she sighed. 'So, we have to keep going with them, then?'

'You really don't have a choice here, Breanna. Thomas needs these exercises to develop proper strength in his neck.' Kate didn't want to alarm the young mother that if neglected, Thomas's present problem could have far-reaching effects, like him not being able to move his head and face normally.

Breanna bit her lip. 'He cries…'

'He will for a time,' Kate said gently. 'But eventually he'll resist less when the muscle begins to relax and his little body becomes more in tune. It's unfortunate this has happened to your baby, Breanna, but you need to devote yourself entirely to his needs for the moment.'

'I do want to help him.' Breanna stared down at the perfect features of her little boy.

'I'm sure you do,' Kate said. 'So, as well as his exercises, make little changes to his environment where you can. Babies can get bored too,' she added with a smile.

Breanna frowned a bit, pushing a tendril of fair hair behind her ear. 'Like...moving the furniture around? That would be a real pain.'

'It would,' Kate agreed. 'But you don't need to go that far. Just do small practical things like alternating the ends when you place him in his cot so he's looking out from a different position. And if you change arms when you hold him so he's not always lying on the same side, that will encourage him to move his head as well.'

'OK...that sounds good.' Breanna perked up. 'What about some tummy time? Is he too young?'

'It's fine as long as there's always someone there to supervise. And if he has trouble lifting his head, you could roll a small towel into a crescent shape and position it underneath his chest. Put some colourful little toys in front of him as well so that he's more likely to want to focus.'

Breanna grimaced slightly. 'There's so much to think about, isn't there?'

'And it will take up a large chunk of your time, Breanna. But you can do it,' Kate said bracingly. 'Do you have family support?'

'Uh-huh, that's why we moved back to Mt Pryde. Brad and I are a team and we have his mum and my mum. They both came to the physio with us so they could learn the exercises.'

'That's good to hear.' Kate looked down at her hands now bare of any rings. Thomas was a very lucky little boy. He had both his mum and dad to care for him. Something Luke and Mia didn't have any longer. She pulled her thoughts quickly away from self-pity and smiled at Breanna. 'Thomas looks peaceful so we won't disturb him but any time you're worried, don't hesitate to come in. And keep up regular visits to the child health clinic, won't you?'

'I will.' Breanna stood and then leaned down to lift the baby capsule with its sleeping occupant. 'Thanks, Dr Preston,' she added shyly. 'You've been great.'

* * *

Kate didn't know how she got through the rest of the week. Perhaps it was more good luck than good management that she'd avoided Aiden. But, then, maybe he'd been avoiding her as well, she conceded thinly.

It helped that her list had been light so that she'd managed an early getaway each afternoon. But now it was Friday. He'd be at the staff meeting this afternoon.

Her musing stopped abruptly when her phone rang and Vicky said, 'Kate, I've just had a call from the after-hours clinic. One of the on-call doctors can't do his shift this weekend—family crisis or something. They're wondering whether we could supply someone. Would you be free, by any chance?'

Kate thought quickly. Her parents were coming into town tomorrow for their fortnightly shop and Kate had arranged to meet them for lunch. But she was certain they wouldn't mind coming earlier and collecting the children for the weekend.

Luke and Mia would love it and it would give

Kate a chance to show she really could pull her weight in the practice. 'Yes, I could manage that, Vicky.'

'Brilliant. I'll let them know.'

'Oh—before you go,' Kate said hurriedly. 'Who else is covering, do you know?'

'Hang on, I have the lists right here in front of me. Oh, you're lucky. You'll be with Aiden.'

Kate's tummy clenched. Her nerve ends twanged. 'Aiden?'

'Mmm. It's a nine-thirty start. Is that OK?'

'Fine.' Kate's voice was hardly there and she put the phone down.

CHAPTER FOUR

KATE saw her last patient out. As the time for the staff meeting had ticked by, she'd begun to feel almost ill with nerves. But at least Angelo and Brady would be there as a buffer.

Surely if she took an adult approach to the situation with Aiden, they could work together co-operatively. Surely.

Taking her compact from her bag, she went across to the window and began a few running repairs on her make-up, finally freshening her lip gloss. When the rap sounded on her door, she spun round, the tube still in her hand. 'Yes?'

'Kate?'

Aiden. Her heart sped up its rhythm. 'Come in,' she called, stuffing her make-up back into her bag, steadying herself as the door opened and Aiden poked his head in.

'Staff meeting's rescheduled for Monday,' he said shortly. 'Executive decision.'

'Oh.' Kate looked disconcerted. 'Does this happen often?'

'Now and again for various reasons.'

'And no one thought to tell me?'

'Hey, I'm only the messenger.'

Kate gripped the back of her chair, unnerved by his abrupt tone, and his eyes were so hard to read. She beckoned him in.

He threw her a quick burning glance. 'Are you quite sure?' They both knew exactly what the other was thinking.

Kate stood her ground. 'Come in, Aiden.' They had to have this conversation some time. It may as well be now.

Aiden came in and planted himself against the wall, noticing her distracted manner, the firm press of her lips. And in a flash he knew he had to take a step back here. Kate Preston wasn't someone he could pursue a light affair with. She had responsibilities way above the norm, including a huge commitment to her children. It was time he looked at the wider picture. He lifted a shoulder in a tight shrug. 'You first, then.'

Kate's chin came up. Her heart was hammering and she was unnerved by how watchful he seemed. 'All right.' She sucked in a quick breath. 'Obviously, we need to talk about what happened here on Monday.'

His eyes narrowed. 'If you want an apology—'

'I don't! I'm a grown woman, Aiden. I could have stopped you. I didn't.'

'Oh, boy…' Aiden took a huge breath that filled his diaphragm and lifted his shoulders. Taking a few steps, he mock-sagged against the corner of her desk. 'I thought you might have had me done for sexual harassment.'

'Oh, please.' Kate laughed unwillingly. 'You do love your drama, don't you, Doctor?'

'I've packaged it. I was reared with three younger sisters. Drama was dished up with dinner.'

Kate rolled her eyes, feeling relief as tangible as the walls around her. 'In reality, I suspect you were an indulgent big brother.'

He pretended outrage. 'Hey, I was always at their beck and call. I still am even now.'

'OK.' Kate held up a hand in retreat. 'I'll just have to take your word for that.'

A breath of silence and a moment of deep awareness that startled them both.

'So…' Kate rubbed her hands down the sides of her trousers. 'No meeting, then. I guess we can go home.'

'Or we could get out of the place and go for a coffee somewhere.' Aiden looked at his watch. 'You don't need to pick up the kids for a while, do you?'

'No.' Being Friday, Luke and Mia were in after-school care. And it had been an age since she'd done anything without the kids in tow. Still Kate hesitated. She felt slightly pushed again yet she didn't want to appear unfriendly just when they'd more or less restored some element of ease to their relationship. She decided to compromise.'I guess I could manage that, as long as we don't take too long.'

'We'll go to the country club. They have an

amazing alfresco area and the best coffee in town.'

'All right if I have tea?'

'They serve the best tea as well,' he promised, the need to be with her unexpectedly dragging at his heart. And out of the blue he felt as though he was in a foreign country, stepping on ground he'd never traversed before.

'Oh, this is amazing, isn't it?' Kate exclaimed as they entered the huge pavilion at the rear of the club. Already there were people about, enjoying the outdoor areas. Aiden was a member and had signed her in. Perhaps she should join, Kate thought, already eyeing the pool for the children and a blue foamy spa that was obviously for the adults.

'Mt Pryde's locked into the tourist dollar now,' Aiden said. 'The natural scenery is a huge draw card for climbers and trekkers. And for the day trippers who just want to enjoy a slower pace, eat somewhere nice, buy some local products.'

'Mt Pryde is a gem,' Kate agreed. 'I fell in love

with the place when I came for my interview at the practice.'

Aiden tilted his head, his eyes unexpectedly soft. 'Falling in love is good.'

They smiled at each other.

Then hastily looked away.

'I'll go and order.' Aiden guided Kate towards a table beside a wall of flowering shrubs. 'What about something to eat?'

'Oh—yes, please. Something luscious and decadently sweet. I'm in need of an energy hit.'

'You've got it.' He grinned. 'Leave it to me.'

Her gaze thoughtful, Kate watched him make his way through the courtyard tables. He had a fantastic body, perfectly proportioned to his height. No wonder he excelled at the physical pursuits he engaged in.

She gave an impatient little shake of her head. Why was her body betraying her like this? Maybe it was having a joke at her expense. She just wished she wasn't so unnervingly fascinated by everything about Aiden O'Connor.

From his ridiculously long lashes to the tiny cleft in his chin.

She puzzled anew about his personal life. One she knew nothing about. Did he have a love interest? A lover? Maybe he was an opportunist. Was she being terribly gullible? She gave a little huff of exasperation.

'Here we are.'

'Aiden.' Kate gave a little jump. She'd been miles away.

'That's me.' His mouth tucked in at the corners. He put down the tray and began unloading their food on to the table.

'Wow!' Kate's eyes widened. 'Lemon meringue pie!'

'You don't like it?' Aiden looked pained.

'You're kidding!' She gave a half-laugh. 'I love it. And you've got ice cream as well.'

'Sprung.' The smile he shot her was slow and lazy. 'And if you don't care for it, I'll manage both lots.'

She chuckled. 'You'll put on weight.'

'Not me.' Aiden took up his fork and scooped up a mouthful of his pie.

Oh, heavens, he was so physical! Kate's heart clattered as she watched him sink his teeth into the shortcrust pastry.

'I gather we're rostered together at the after-hours clinic tomorrow.'

Kate dragged her eyes away to concentrate. 'Vicki asked me to fill in. Tell me about the set-up. Where is it and what kinds of cases do we treat?'

Aiden obliged. 'The clinic is an initiative of the local council set up to take pressure off the casualty department at the hospital. It's attached to the hospital building but quite separate in its operation. And no need to bring a packed lunch.' A quick smile dusted his mouth. 'We have an open invitation to eat at the hospital canteen. As for cases, expect anything from headaches to hangovers.'

Kate's eyebrows arched 'So, just a regular day at the surgery, then?'

'Usually. But as we both know know, in our

job, emergencies can and do happen. And in this particular region, rock climbers and bush walkers are notorious for getting into trouble.'

At the thought, Kate felt the prickle of an old fear rise up to rock her hard-won confidence. Suddenly, she was pitched back to another place and time. Another emergency. The one that had taken the life of her children's father; when the certainty of her life had been snuffed out as quickly and irrevocably as a candle in the wind.

Resolutely, she picked up her cup and took a mouthful of hot, fragrant tea. She'd be OK. This was a different time and place. She'd worked in the ER in the States, for heaven's sake. And been good at it. It had only been after Cory's accident she'd switched to family medicine, deciding she wanted a slower pace and more predictability in her daily work.

Suddenly, out of the blue, she sensed an urgent need in herself, one only the nearness of her children would assuage. It was as though she needed to reconnect them as a family. Hug the sweet warmth of their little bodies close. And it couldn't wait. 'Aiden, the food is lovely but I'm going to eat and run, if you don't mind.'

'Was it something I said?'

'Of course not. Luke and Mia will be waiting and it's a bit of a drive back to town.'

'It's barely a kilometre,' Aiden pointed out. 'Ten minutes tops.' Something was wrong and he didn't know what.

Kate finished most of her pie but left the ice cream. When she got to her feet, Aiden swung up as well.

'I'll come with you.'

Kate retrieved her bag and slung it over her shoulder. 'No need.'

'Hey, you don't expect me to sit here on my own, do you?.' With his hand unobtrusively on the small of her back, Aiden guided her out of the building. When they got to her car, he turned her to face him. 'Kate, is everything OK? Talk to me if it'll help.'

'Everything's…fine,' she faltered.

Aiden frowned. He had his doubts about that.

'Look, we're friends, aren't we? Friends look out for one another.'

Kate wanted to take off, to turn and run from the look of concern in his eyes, but it was oddly compelling. She shook her head. This wouldn't do at all. 'I just want to be with my kids, Aiden. It's about as complicated as that.'

He raised an eyebrow. 'I'll follow you back to town, then. OK if I swing by the school with you and say hello to Luke and Mia?'

'Of course.' Kate's voice was barely there. Something shifted within her. What else could she say?

Keeping Kate's Lexus in sight, Aiden adjusted his sunglasses . They were driving in a westerly direction back to town and the setting sun was like a ball of fire over the horizon, making driving visibility more difficult than usual. He'd gathered Kate was still getting used to local driving conditions and had warned her to keep her speed down. Thank heaven, she seemed to be adhering to his advice.

With a country road that needed constant maintenance, Aiden had learned to be ever vigilant. Kangaroos and wallabies darted out of nowhere at any time. Add idiot drivers to the mix and you had accidents waiting to happen. And he certainly didn't want anything happening to Kate.

'Sheesh!' Aiden was jolted out of his introspection as a farm utility shot out of a side road and right into Kate's path. For a split second he forgot to breathe, his stomach knotted and then relief in the form of an expletive left his mouth. Kate had reacted like a pro driver and accelerated away, avoiding what had seemed an inevitable crash. *Attagirl.*

Aiden's relief was short-lived. The ute had too much speed. It had shot across the centre line, putting it directly on a collision course with an oncoming car. 'Fool,' he muttered. 'Bloody, bloody fool.'

Oh, dear God. Horror-stricken, Kate followed the vehicle's trajectory in her rear-vision mirror as it plunged out of control across the central traffic island. Mechanically, she cut back her speed. The crash was inevitable.

It took only a few mind-numbing seconds for the doctor in her to respond. She brought her car to a swift halt and then began reversing back along the shoulder of the road towards the accident scene.

In seconds, she was out of the car, grabbing her bag and running.

Aiden popped the tailgate of his Land Rover and pulled out his medical kit, complete with oxygen. He was the designated MO for the skydiving team. He needed a fully stocked kit always at the ready. He pushed out a long breath through his mouth, adrenalin surging into his veins as he sprinted towards the crashed vehicles.

And then he saw Kate running from the opposite direction. He hadn't time to process the implications but he was glad, very glad she was there.

'What do we have?' Kate was slightly out of breath, her heart drumming.

'From what I can see, there's only one occupant in each of the vehicles. I'll take the ute. Can you check on the other one, please?'

'Have you called the emergency services?'

'Yes. Go! Do what you can.'

Kate ran. She sized up the situation in seconds. The impact of the crash had sent both vehicles careering off the the road so that they were now facing in opposite directions. It was obvious the driver's door on the car had been pushed in. She'd have to get access to her patient through the passenger side. She moved quickly. Blocking out the sun, she cupped her hands around her eyes and peered inside the car. The driver was slumped over the steering-wheel.

Fortunately, it was an older-type vehicle without a central locking system. Kate rapped on the window and the driver lifted his head. She saw he was parchment pale, obviously shocked to bits. Kate gestured towards the door. The man seemed to register. His seat belt was still holding but he managed to release it and then inch himself across to pop open the lock. Kate swung the door open. 'I'm Kate, I'm a doctor,' she said. 'Are you hurt?'

The man stared uncomprehendingly. Kate asked again, 'Are you hurt?'

He shook his head ever so slightly and winced. Whiplash for sure, Kate thought, and no wonder. But it seemed he'd been lucky.

'Car's a write-off,' the man said, and gave a weak, hollow laugh. 'I thought I was a goner.'

'Yes,' Kate said, and suppressed a shudder. 'I saw it happen. Now, just stay put and I'll check you over.'

Kate began a quick neuro assessment, relieved to see the man's pupils were equal and reacting. 'What's your name?' she asked, gauging the state of her patient's competency.

'Gary Neumann…I work for the council. Just on me way home and this happens.'

'Squeeze my fingers really hard, please, Gary. Great, that's good.'

Gary's teeth began chattering. 'Am I gonna be all right, Doc…?'

'I can't tell you that, Gary. You'll need to go

to the hospital and be checked out thoroughly.' Kate listened to the man's chest and checked for rib injuries. 'In the meantime, I'll try to make you more comfortable and then it's just a case of waiting until the ambulance gets here. Now, someone I can call for you?'

'Bethany, my wife.' He looked helplessly around. 'Mobile's in the glove-box.'

Which was now totally inaccessible from the force of the crash. Kate pulled out her own phone. 'I'll call her for you. Can you remember her number?'

'Yep,' Gary croaked. 'She'll still be at work in town.'

Kate paused with her finger over the dial pad. 'So she could meet you at the hospital, right?'

'Reckon. Go easy, Doc, She'll get a fright…'

'Relax, Gary,' Kate reassured him gently. 'I won't alarm her.'

Aiden meanwhile had his own problems. The force of the crash had peeled back the mud-guards on the front of the utility, causing them to be firmly wedged against the cabin doors.

Aiden gritted his teeth, straining as he tried to force the bent metal away from the doorhandle. Useless. He swore, thumping the metal with the heel of his hand. He needed a tool of some kind. Tyre lever, he decided in a flash, and ran back to his own vehicle. Using every bit of strength he had, he finally forced the door open.

'Hells bells,' Aiden murmured, recognising one of his older patients, Walter Hemmant. He was slumped back against the the seat. 'Wal?' Aiden put his hand on the man's cartoid pulse. 'What gives, mate?'

Walter shook his head and said hoarsely, 'Dunno, Doc.'

'OK. Talk to me Wal. Any numbness in your hands or face?'

Walter's pale blue eyes regarded Aiden confusedly. 'Don't feel any. I had a fair bit of speed up…running late for a meeting in town. I went for the brakes…couldn't get enough pressure from my feet. Then the ute just bolted away from me. It all happened in a flash.'

While his patient was speaking, Aiden was

doing his own assessment. There was no slurring in the older man's speech so no indication of stroke. 'Wal, can you move your legs for me?'

Walter struggled for a second and then said defeatedly, 'Can't move 'em, Doc. They're jammed under the console.'

'All right, don't force anything,' Aiden said urgently. 'Already he could see the red stain of blood seeping from beneath Wally's light-coloured trousers and the metallic smell was beginning to infiltrate the air in the cabin.

Aiden moved in quick precision. Could be a busted femoral artery. Or not. He hoped *not*. 'Wal, I'm going to pop an oxygen mask on you. It'll help you over the shock you're feeling. Just breathe in and out normally. Good man. Now, I need to pack a dressing around your thigh. We can't do any more until the fire brigade gets here. They'll have some equipment to free your leg.'

'Need some help here?'

'Kate.' Aiden's head head jerked round. 'How's your patient?'

'Nothing broken, as far as I could see. Bit shocky. Do you have a spare oxygen cylinder?'

'No, sorry.' Aiden made a mental note to include an extra unit in his kit for future use and went on packing Walter's thigh.

'What about a collar?' Kate's voice was crisp and she realised she'd reached a new plateau of calm, enabling her mind to become sharp and practical.

'In the kit. Help yourself.'

'Thanks.' Kate dug around and then held up the located item. 'I'll be right back.'

Aiden swore silently with frustration. Wally's leg needed a tourniquet urgently but there was no way he could gain proper access until the metal holding his leg had been cut away.

'Right.' Kate was back. 'What do you need?'

'See if you can get an IV in,' Aiden was brisk. 'I have to try to keep pressure on the leg. This is Wally. He's actually one of my patients.'

'Running late for surgery hours, was he?'

'Seems like it.' Aiden grinned crookedly, appreciating Kate's dry humour in the tense atmosphere.

'Vein's slow.' Kate's mouth pulled into a tight moue.

'Keep trying. Wally needs all the fluids we can run into him.'

'The paramedics will have haemaccel on board.' Kate felt relief as she finally found a vein plump enough to take the IV needle. 'OK, I'm done here.'

'Thanks.' Aiden cocked his head. 'Is that the cavalry?'

'Almost here, by the sound of it,' Kate said, as the wail of sirens filled the stillness of late afternoon.

With the arrival of the emergency vehicles, things moved into swift, professional rhythm.

'We'll take off with this one, Doc.'

'Thanks, guys.' Kate nodded to the paramedics as Gary was gently extricated from his car and loaded onto a stretcher. 'His wife should be waiting at the hospital.'

Gary raised his hand in a brief farewell salute and then closed his eyes.

Right. That was all she could do here. Kate turned and made her way quickly back to Aiden and the other emergency.

She saw with relief that the fire brigade had arrived and were already assembling the Jaws of Life. The hydraulic equipment would be used to stretch the car's metal and release Wally from the crippling pressure on his leg. 'Aiden?' Kate moved in closer.

'Kate.' Aiden craned his head around the tangle of equipment being positioned.

'Need a second pair of hands?' Silly question. Of course he didn't. The paramedics were standing by to provide back-up. There was no need for her to stay.

'Take off,' Kate.' Aiden's voice roughened. 'Go and pick up your kids.'

But for reasons she couldn't explain, Kate stayed, flinching when the buzzing whine of the hydraulic motor shattered the stillness of country quiet.

'We're about to rip into it, Doc,' one of the fire officers shouted above the din. 'You'd better wear one of these.' Reaching over, he planted a safety hat on Aiden's head. 'Right, lads, crack 'er open. And gentle as you can, OK?'

Kate couldn't believe how quickly it was all done. But, then, these men were professionals, brilliant at what they did. In a matter of a few minutes Wally, tourniquet in place and tucked under a space blanket, was being lifted and carried across to the waiting ambulance.

Holding the drip with the plasma expander, Aiden followed the stretcher. With his patient safely aboard, he turned and saw Kate. He frowned. What the hell? He jogged back to where she was waiting near the crashed utility. 'Kate, you didn't have to hang about.'

'I know. I…just wanted to make sure you were OK.'

'I wasn't the one in the accident.'

Embarrassed, Kate force a laugh. 'I can look out for my colleague, can't I?'

Aiden sent her a puzzled look. Hell, was there a subtext here? 'You should be with your children.'

'Just going.' In a whirlpool of confusion, Kate

teetered on the edge of telling him that for the first time in the longest time it wasn't just her children she wanted. For the last three years she'd made them her top priority, her life. Now, hardly without her being aware of it, a whole new world had opened up and suddenly she had choices.

Aiden began gathering up the medical debris, stuffing it into a plastic bag and securing the zip-lock at the top. Seeing Kate still waiting had rattled him. She'd ambushed him out of the blue. It puzzled him.

'I'm heading to the hospital,' he told her. 'I want to follow through on Wally.'

'Oh—OK.' So he wasn't coming to the school with her. Of course he wasn't. He was a doctor, for heaven's sake, his patient would have to come first.

'Kate?' Aiden's dark brows snapped together. 'Is there something else?'

She shook her head. 'I won't hold you up any longer.'

'See you tomorrow, then. Sorry I can't get to say hello to the kids.'

Kate heard the note of regret in his voice. Well, maybe it was genuine and maybe it wasn't. She wasn't sure if she wanted to find out.

CHAPTER FIVE

SATURDAY morning.

Kate's thoughts were all over the place as she slid her car into a parking space at the hospital. She winced, recalling for the umpteenth time the weird kind of awkwardness that had descended between her and Aiden just before they'd left the accident scene yesterday.

Where were they now? she wondered yet again. Why was it all so difficult? She swung impatiently out of the Lexus and locked the door. She needed no preoccupation today. She had a clinic to run.

He was cutting it fine. Aiden sprinted up the ramp at the entrance to the hospital and waited for the notoriously-slow electronic front door to chug open and admit him. He could see Kate through the plate-glass panel. She was propped against the counter at Reception, hovering over some paperwork. Her hair was up, softly constrained, and in a mad gesture of machismo he wanted to stride forward and set it free, thread his fingers through its lustre and steady her head whilst he kissed her.

He gave a roll of his eyes. Idiot. He had to keep his feet on the ground here. Maybe Kate was in his future. Maybe not. All he knew for certain was that he wanted her to think well of him.

Kate looked up as he approached, feeling the slight flutter and jerk of her breathing. 'Good morning,' she said quietly when he moved in beside her.

'And to you.' He breathed in the flowery scent of her shower gel, his blue gaze flaring and then softening over her. 'Rosie clued you in?' Rosemary Finch was the receptionist at the clinic.

'And given me the tour. How's Wally?' Kate asked.

'Stable. They're running some tests this morning. That might tell us something. I'll pop up to the ward when I get a minute. What about your chap?'

Kate shrugged. 'When I rang last night to check, he'd already been released.'

'Excellent.' Aiden signed the attendance book and closed it. Turning his head, he sent her a very sweet smile. 'Ready to rock and roll, then?'

Kate gathered up her paperwork. 'That's what we're here for.'

Leaving Reception, they turned left and made their way along a short corridor to the two adjoining consulting rooms.

'Care to meet up for lunch?' Aiden asked, pausing outside his door.

Kate looked uncertain. 'Is there time?'

'You bet. Officially we're closed for an hour from twelve-thirty. They don't overload us here, Kate. Relax. Walk in the park.'

But far from being a walk in the park, as Aiden had predicted, his clinic had been wall to wall, as one patient after another had trooped in. He gave himself a mental ticking-off when he saw out his final patient before the lunch-break.

He should have remembered the seasonal workers, the pickers for the various small crops, were in town, and injuries like blisters, backache and sunburn were high on the list of complaints. He'd imagine Kate's list had been full as well. Kate. He felt the sudden leap in his pulse. He was so looking forward to spending a little down time with her, sharing a meal with her…

'Aiden?' Rosemary tapped and stuck her head in. 'Got a minute?'

'Yep.' Aiden waved her in. He finished his notes on his last patient and looked up. 'What's up, Rosie?'

'Sorry—I know it's lunchtime but there's a patient in Reception. A young woman. I think she needs to be seen.'

'O-K….' Aiden pushed his chair back and waited.

'She's jerky, stressed. I think if I asked her to come back this afternoon, she wouldn't.'

'Right.' Aiden trusted Rosie's instincts totally. 'Show her in, then. Do we have a name?'

'Leanne Taylor. I doubt she's a local.'

Aiden nodded. Probably another picker. 'I'll handle it from here, Rosie. Thanks.'

Leanne Taylor gave a furtive look around before taking a seat at Aiden's request.

Aiden considered his patient briefly, agreeing with Rosie's observation that the woman's body language spelled flight. He injected what he hoped were calm and professionalism into his query. 'What can I do for you, Ms Taylor?'

'It's Leanne,' she said, barely audibly. 'I've burned my hand…' The young woman looked down at her hand lying palm up on her lap.

Aiden dropped onto a stool and swung closer. He began loosening the home-made bandage. 'Ouch!' he said under his breath as he looked at the injury. 'That looks nasty. When did you do this?'

'Couple of days ago. I…um…dunked it into some hot water by mistake.'

Hot water be damned, Aiden thought darkly,

looking at the configuration of the burned skin. This had been no accident. Leanne's hand had been deliberately held under *boiling* water. Her natural reaction would have been to make a fist to protect her skin, thus causing the zebra-striped pattern on her palm. He felt anger swirl in his gut. Why was this still happening? They were supposed to be living in enlightened times. These days women had choices. They didn't have to put up with this kind of abuse.

'It's on the way to being infected, Leanne. Why don't you tell me what really happened?' Aiden hoped his tone was gentle enough to draw a response from his patient.

There was a moment of tense silence, a moment when Aiden almost felt his patient's capitulation. But then a shadow came over her face and her lips remained tightly closed.

'I can help you, Leanne. You only have to ask.'

'It's no big deal. I just need you to fix my hand. I have to get b-back.'

Aiden's mouth drew in. Underneath Leanne's small attempt at bravado, he sensed a fear so tangible he could have all but captured it and bottled it. So he was on the right track. But he'd need to be very careful if he had any hope of getting the outcome he wanted and Leanne desperately needed. 'I'll prescribe some antibiotics for you.' He went back to the computer. 'Are you with the pickers?' he asked, while he waited for the printout.

Leanne nodded and kept her head down.

'Must be difficult keeping children's schooling going when you have to move around so much. But maybe you don't have children?' Aiden flipped out the prescription, signed it and handed to Leanne with a questioning half-smile.

'I do. Kyton, he's eight.' Leanne held the script to her chest. 'He lives with my mum in Brisbane. I can't have him with me.'

'And why is that, Leanne?'

The girl's face came up. 'I'm with Wayne now—there's no room for Ky in the caravan.'

'You must miss him.'

Leanne nodded and blinked rapidly. 'But Wayne says…'

'Wayne says?' Aiden waited.

'He's not Ky's dad. He doesn't see why he should have him around.'

'That doesn't seem very kind, does it?' Aiden's tone hardened as he thought of his patient's injury. 'In fact, Wayne doesn't sound very kind at all.'

Leanne darted a scared look towards the door. 'He's…OK. Most of the time. And he's always sorry after…'

Aren't they all? Aiden's mouth twisted. 'The burn to your hand was no accident, was it, Leanne?'

Leanne bowed her head. The silence stretched. Until…

'I forgot to buy Wayne's cigarettes. He got mad.' Leanne's throat trembled as she swallowed. 'I'd just boiled water to do the washing-up. I was pouring it into the sink when he grabbed me from behind…'

'It's all right, Leanne.' Aiden said gently, pushing a box of tissues towards the girl and waiting while she blotted her eyes. 'Don't go on. I get the picture.' When his patient had settled, he asked, 'How did you get here this morning?'

'I got a lift with one of the other women from the caravan park,' she responded throatily. 'Wayne always hits the drink on Friday night. He was still asleep. But he'll be OK when he wakes.'

Until the next time. Aiden gave in to a silent venting of anger. His jaw tightened. He had options here. One, he could hand the prescription to his patient and let her go. He would have done his duty as a health professional. Or he could try to save Leanne from a situation from which she obviously couldn't save herself. In other words, stick his nose in. He shrugged inwardly. He had to try. 'When we're finished here, Leanne, do you *really* want to go back to the caravan park? And the kind of crappy life you seem to have with Wayne?'

There was a long silence, the atmosphere so still, Aiden could feel the rise and fall of his own chest, in and out. So much depended on these next few moments.

'What choice do I have?' Leanne sent an agonised look at the doctor treating her.

'There are steps we can take,' Aiden said with quiet authority. 'What we call protocols. If you want help to get out of your abusive relationship, then we begin with the first step. You report Wayne to the police for assault.'

Leanne gasped. 'I couldn't do that!'

Aiden wasn't surprised at his patient's reaction. Leanne was running scared and who could blame her? 'If you can't do that, then you have to put some distance between you.'

'Leave town?'

'That would be by far the best option. Could you go to your mother's?'

'He'd find me.'

'Then I can give you the address of a women's shelter where you'll be safe until you sort yourself out. It's up to you, Leanne. What do you want to do? If you decide you want out, we have to act now. There's a bus leaving for Brisbane within the hour. You could be on it.'

'I...' Leanne took a ragged breath and then another.

'What about your boy? Don't you think he needs his mum?' Aiden knew he was pushing hard. Perhaps too hard. If he blew it now...

Leanne squeezed her eyes shut as though she had the mother of all headaches, and it seemed an eternity before she flicked them open. 'If you think I can get away, I'll do it...'

Aiden felt a gush of relief whistle silently from between his lips. He took his wallet from his back pocket and slipped out a business card. Turning it over, he scribbled something on the back and handed to his patient. 'That's the address of the shelter. They'll steer you in the right direction.' Flipping the card back over, he said, 'This is how you can contact me. If for any reason, you need verification that you sought medical attention for your injured hand, I'm available to give my findings.'

Looking as though she couldn't believe the speed at which things were happening, Leanne took the card and tucked it into the little fob pocket on her polo shirt. 'OK.' She bit her bottom lip to stop it trembling. 'Thank you…'

'No need for thanks, Leanne. Just doing my job.' But Aiden knew he'd done far more than was expected of him. And pushed where perhaps he shouldn't. But this young woman was barely into her twenties. A victim of making the wrong choice in a relationship. If she held firm now, she had the chance to make something of her life. And if ever he ran into that pond scum, Wayne, he'd shove him up against the wall and… Aiden's fist curled and then uncurled slowly. Violence bred violence. There was no way he was going down that path.

'Right.' He got to his feet. 'We'll buzz you round to Casualty now and get a proper dressing put on your hand. While we're there, I'll pick up some antibiotics from the dispensary. You can get the script filled later. Do you have money?'

Leanne nodded. 'A little.'

'Enough to get your bus ticket?'

'Yes. I had some Wayne doesn't know about.

And I still have my mobile. Oh.' Leanne stared up at him uncertainly. 'I don't have my clothes.'

'Clothes can be replaced, Leanne.' Aiden's voice was firm. 'Your health and safety are far more important. Now, as soon as we're done here, I'll drive you across town to the bus station.'

Kate chose a vegetable bake for her lunch. She was pleasantly surprised to see the canteen was bright and cheerful and the food looked freshly prepared.

Aiden hadn't yet arrived so she found a table near the window that looked out over the hospital gardens. Tucking into her food, she felt lighter than she had in days. Was it the prospect of Aiden's company for lunch? she wondered. She stifled a huff of irritation. *For pity's sake, am I that needy?*

'Hi,' a woman said chirpily beside her. 'Are you Kate?'

Startled, Kate's head came up. 'Yes, I'm Kate.'

'Fliss O'Byrne.'

'Oh—you're Jo's friend,' Kate smiled.

'Mmm. We trained together. Jo told me to look out for you. I'm doing a shift in Casualty today. Mind if I join you?'

Kate twitched a hand in invitation. 'Please.'

Fliss set her tray on the table and slid into the vacant chair opposite. 'I had a peek at the roster for the after-hours clinic and saw your name. Figured I might catch you here in the lunch-break. How's it been? Busy?'

'Fairly,' Kate said. 'You?'

'Swarming.' Fliss picked up her fork. 'Start of the picking season. I even had one young guy with a *hammy.*'

Kate raised a brow. 'Hamstring?'

'Mmm.' Fliss chuckled. I straightened him out. It was fun—well, not for him. I used to work in sports medicine. Piece of cake.' Fliss hardly stopped for breath. 'I see we've both chosen the same meal. The food's consistently good here.' Her mouth turned up in a quick smile. 'I had lunch here with Callum on my very first day. Seems ages ago now.'

'And now you're married to Callum.' Kate's mouth quirked. 'Jo mentioned you'd had a whirlwind romance.'

Fliss gurgled a laugh. 'I guess we did,' she said easily. 'And now we have a gorgeous baby boy. You have kids, don't you, Kate?'

'I do. Luke is eight and Mia six.'

'You're kidding! You don't look old enough.'

Kate rolled her eyes. 'Oh, believe me, I am. How old is your little boy?'

'Flynn is ten months.' Fliss looked misty. 'He's very sweet.'

'So, are you back at work full time?' Kate asked interestedly.

'Uh-uh. Just doing the odd shift when they're short-staffed. I'm in no hurry to increase my hours.'

Kate picked up her glass of water and took a mouthful. What a nice option to have, she thought with a touch of envy.

They continued their meal, their conversation general, until Fliss asked cheekily, 'You keep looking towards the door, Kate. Expecting someone?'

'Not really.' Kate feigned disinterest. 'Aiden O'Connor is on duty with me today. He mentioned meeting for lunch. He must have got caught up.' *Or thought better of his invitation.*

'He's seriously edible, isn't he?' Fliss's tone was wickedly conspiratorial. 'And available.'

'Is he?' Kate swallowed the sudden dryness in her throat. 'I had the impression that perhaps Aiden had a girlfriend in Brisbane.'

'Oh, surely the grapevine would have picked up on that little morsel.' Fliss was dismissive. 'Mind you, he's never been short of a date when we've had our social gatherings. And why would he be? He's single and gorgeous. Oh, that's me.' She looked at her pager and whirled to her feet. 'Darn, I was enjoying this.' She gave a quick lift of her dark brows.'Let's catch up for coffee soon.'

'That'd be nice.' And it would be, Kate thought. Fliss was warm and vibrant and fun. She had a lightness about her that was catching. It would be good to have another friend in Mt Pryde. 'Give me a call at the surgery.'

'Will do. Ah.' Fliss glanced towards the door and gave a throaty chuckle. 'Here's your man at last.'

Well, he wasn't *her* man by any stretch of the imagination, Kate thought, watching Aiden stop and exchange a few words with Fliss and then make his way over to her table.

'Sorry to bale on you.' He slid into the chair vacated by Fliss. 'Involved consult.'

'And it's taken up most of your break.' Kate gestured to the take-away coffee he was cradling. 'Is that all you're having?'

'I'm fine,' he dismissed shortly. 'How was your morning?' Aiden took a mouthful of his coffee.

'Well, obviously better than yours. Would you like to debrief later?' Kate offered.

He looked up. 'Maybe. I'll let you know.'

His eyes held a remoteness Kate hadn't seen before. She knew instinctively that something was wrong. Involved consult, he'd said. 'Look,' she invited, making a throw-away motion with her hand. 'I plan to do something quick and easy for dinner tonight. Come round. No pressure—just unwind.'

Their eyes met and his slid away. 'Thanks for the offer, Kate. But I think I need to go for a long run around the paddock after work, slough off this foul mood.'

'And that's going to take you all night?' Kate stood her ground, her manner resolute.

Aiden lifted the coffee to his mouth. He must be nuts. Why hadn't he jumped at the chance to spend some quality time with her? His gut clenched. Hell, she looked so fresh and feminine, sweetly pretty in her print dress that outlined the soft curve of her breasts and swirled away to fall in soft folds almost to her ankles. 'I realise you want to help, Kate…'

'Then let me.' Kate shook her head in consternation. 'You mentioned an involved consult. How involved?'

He lifted a shoulder. 'Messy.' And he didn't

particularly want to go there. Not after the way it had turned out.

'Are you doubting your handling of it?' Kate asked with some perception.

In spades. He laughed without humour. 'Sometimes I wonder why I took on family medicine. Maybe I should have taken the option to train as a surgeon. Sew 'em up and ship 'em out.'

'And that, O'Connor, is a copout. From what I've seen, you're a fine doctor.'

'Yeah.'

Kate rolled her eyes. 'Aiden, you can only do what you can for patients. What they'll *allow* you to do.'

He gulped down the rest of his coffee and plonked the empty carton back on the table. 'And that about sums it up, doesn't it?'

Kate sensed the frustration behind his remark and backed off a little. She glanced at her watch. 'Time we were getting back. Rosie said if we're not too busy this afternoon, we'll close early. Any stragglers can go round to Casualty.'

'Sounds like a plan.'

His mouth lifted in a token smile and Kate decided there was nothing more to say. At least for now.

Kate drove home. They'd finished early but Aiden for reasons of his own had already left the clinic when she'd gone to sign off.

Well, if he was sending her a message to mind her own business, she'd got it. She slid her car into the garage. She could manage quite well without his company. She'd indulge herself, have a bubble bath and phone her kids for starters.

Time sure flew when you were having fun, Kate thought wryly some time later, as she stepped from the bath and towelled herself dry. She pulled on lightweight cotton trousers and a black T-shirt. And who cared if it was faded and old? She wasn't dressing for company.

In the kitchen, she took a bottle of wine from the fridge and poured a generous glass. She'd make a nice dinner, even if she had to dine alone.

She'd just assembled her ingredients on the

counter when the doorbell pealed. Who in the world…?

'Coming,' she called, making her way along the hallway. The sensor light came on as she opened the front door.

'Aiden.' Kate's hushed voice hung in the air. He'd come after all. Just the sight of him had her heart beating double time. He was wearing a snug-fitting white T-shirt that emphasised the tanned nature of his skin and every muscle in his torso—if she was looking, which she was. His cargo-style pants rode low on his hips and his hands were jammed in the back pockets, dragging them lower.

'Hi.' He gave her a ruefully-crooked grin. 'You were right. I've decided my own company stinks. So here I am.'

'So you are.' They were the only words Kate could process in the beat of silence that followed. She lifted a hand, her fingers slowly curling on the front of her T-shirt.

'I should have called, I think.' Aiden's tone

was questioning, his uncertain gaze raking her from head to toe.

Kate shook her head. 'It's fine. Come on in.'

'If you're sure…'

Kate gave him a look and held the door open. They went along the hallway into the lounge room. 'Make yourself at home for a minute. I just have to nip out to my herb garden for a handful of mint.'

Aiden looked around, getting an instant feeling of warmth. Two sofas faced one another beside the fireplace, both covered in brightly coloured throws and big soft cushions. Drawings, presumably by Luke and Mia, were tacked at angles to the walls, alongside framed prints of wilderness country. The room was cosy, oddly sheltering. So much in tune with what he knew of Kate.

Almost drawn by a power beyond his control, he stepped closer to a long sideboard, dipping his head to study the family photographs on display. One in particular grabbed his attention. It was of Mia, a much younger Mia on the shoulders of a man he presumed was her father.

She was grasping his chin so that his head was forced up towards her, both of them with mouths wide with laughter. And Luke in front, wedged against his father's legs, sharing the joke, his smile a mile wide.

Aiden felt a ripple of deep distress. Suddenly he felt like an intruder. Kate's other life was all here, a life she'd shared with her children's father, a life they'd shared as a family. No wonder she was so protective of Luke and Mia, of her own feelings.

'Hey, you.' Kate popped her head in, her presence startling him out of his introspection. He looked back over his shoulder, his smile a bit strained. 'I was just looking at your photos.'

'Oh, yes.' She moved closer to the sideboard. 'This one? Cory and the kids.' Her eyes grew soft. 'It's nice, isn't it? It was one of the last ones we took.'

Aiden felt a lump lodge in his throat. How did he respond to that? *Sorry* didn't cut it. In fact, anything he said would be a platitude and he'd guess she'd had enough of those to last a lifetime. 'Kate...'

She shook her head, seeming to divine his discomfort. She held up her hand and waggled her bunch of mint. 'Come on through to the kitchen. I aim to put you to work.'

He shouldn't have come here. That was Aiden's only thought as he followed Kate along the short hallway to the kitchen. Even though she seemed pleased to see him.

But everything had changed now. He felt lost in a welter of unfamiliar emotions. Nothing was straightforward any more. He just knew he couldn't exploit her vulnerability for his own selfish needs. Kate was a keeper.

'Care for a glass of wine?' Kate arranged several cutting boards on the counter top.

Aiden mentally shook himself. He'd better lighten up. 'Uh—do you have any beer?'

'In the fridge. Help yourself. Then you can come and help me here.' Kate gestured to the array of vegetables lined up on the bench. 'All these have to be sliced, diced or shredded.'

'*All* of them?' Aiden looked horrified. 'Couldn't we just chuck a steak on the barbie?'

'No, we couldn't.' Kate gave a breathless little laugh and flicked him on the sleeve of his pristine white T-shirt. 'Open your beer and get ready to take directions, Doctor.'

Aiden gave a rusty chuckle, felt his mood begin to lift. He took a beer from the fridge and twisted the top off. He took a long swallow. 'Kids away for the weekend?'

'With my folks. They'll bring them home tomorrow afternoon. You didn't really expect to find them here, did you?'

'I hadn't thought. But I can see how much planning you must have to do when you're the sole parent and committed to a job.'

'Got it in one. Now, come on. If you want to eat, then you have to help. Them's the rules here.'

'OK, OK.' Aiden held up his hands in mock surrender. 'Where do you want me to start?'

Kate tossed him a can of chickpeas. 'Could you open these please? Then drain them in the colander hanging from that rack over there. Then wash them.'

'With what?' Aiden looked baffled.

'Running water.' Kate's mouth trapped a wry smile. 'Helpless will get you nowhere, O'Connor.'

'Just testing.' He grinned and proceeded to take directions. Although he couldn't keep up with Kate, he realised, watching as she slivered almonds and popped them in a pan to roast, then just as deftly grated the rind from a lime and juiced it. She chopped shallots and grated fresh ginger, trimmed several other vegetables he didn't recognise. 'OK, I've done the mint,' he said proudly, as if he'd just passed a particularly difficult test.

'Oh, well done.' Kate sent him a half-amused look. 'Now do you think you could open that pack of spinach leaves and throw them into a bowl?'

'This one?' Aiden held up the wooden bowl at the end of the counter.

Kate nodded. 'Then chuck everything else in

while I make the dressing.' She took down a jug and mixed lime juice, honey, olive oil and mustard. 'This is all looking good.' She sent him a satisfied smile.

Aiden's stomach grumbled. He'd had nothing substantial since breakfast. 'Uh, Kate?'

'Yes, Aiden?' She stirred her dressing and tasted it. 'What?' she asked when he remained silent.

He looked uncomfortable. 'I…just wondered whether we're having anything more than salad for dinner?'

She gave a rip of laughter. 'Were you thinking you'd have to rush out and buy fish and chips or something?'

Aiden chuckled. It was a lovely warm sound and it made Kate's heart sing. And she realised she was truly happy. Happier than she'd been for the longest time. 'Tell your stomach to stop worrying,' she said. 'I've strips of lamb marinating in the fridge. I just have to stir-fry them and we're done.'

While Kate cooked the meat, Aiden found

place mats and cutlery and set the table. He couldn't remember when he'd enjoyed himself so much. 'That looks fantastic,' he said approvingly when Kate brought the big oval platter to the table.

Kate beamed. 'Let's make it special and have a candle,' she said. 'Except for my parents, you're the first adult I've had to dinner here.'

Aiden's throat tightened, watching while she lit a plump white candle and placed it in the centre of the table. God, she was so lovely. He was going to need the strength of a thousand horses to keep his hands off her for the entire evening. He cleared his throat. 'Can I top up your wine?'

'Mmm, please. And join me, yes?' She looked at him expectantly.

He nodded, like putty in her hands. He was driving but one glass shouldn't put him over the limit.

With their wine poured, they took their places at the table. Kate lifted her glass to his. 'Thanks for coming, Aiden. I haven't had so much fun in ages.'

'And the night's still young.' Aiden couldn't help the words that tumbled out.

Kate's eyes held a soft mistiness. 'So it is,' she said.

CHAPTER SIX

'THAT was wonderful, Kate,' Aiden said when they'd come to the end of their meal.

'It's one of the kids' favourites.' Kate took a mouthful of her wine. 'Although I always leave out the ginger when I make it for them. They don't care for the extra zing.'

Aiden nodded. It had been good coming here after all. A kind of milestone if he really thought about it. Conversationally, they'd covered a lot of ground. Talked about good stuff—getting-to-know-each-other kind of stuff.

'The patient you were concerned about...' Kate looked down, fingering the raised pattern on her glass. 'Do you want to run anything by me?'

Aiden shrugged broad shoulders and leaned back in his chair. 'Young woman, victim of partner abuse.' He sketched the details of Leanne's injury.

'That's appalling.' Kate shook her head. 'Were you able to help her?'

'Well, I thought I had.' He went on to explain what he'd set in motion for Leanne's escape.

Kate watched his body language carefully, saw his jaw tighten. 'She didn't follow through?'

He gave a hard laugh. 'Guessed it in one. When it came to it, she wouldn't get on the damned bus!'

Well, that was disappointing, Kate thought, but hardly enough for his seemingly white-hot angst.

'The whole thing made me sick. I just wanted to find that cretin and belt the daylights out of him—'

'I can understand that, Aiden. But you can't take it so personally.'

'Oh, believe me, I can,' His words were scathing. 'Any male who beats up women is the lowest of the low in my opinion.'

Well, he'd get no argument from her there,

Kate agreed, but there was something she was not getting here. Something that was still tearing Aiden O'Connor apart. She took a punt on feminine intuition and asked, 'Do you want to talk about it?'

His mouth twisted in a wry smile. 'That obvious, is it?'

Kate merely nodded. 'Tell me, if it'll help.'

In a kind of releasing gesture, Aiden raised his hands, ploughing his fingers through his hair and locking them at the back of his neck. 'A while back, my youngest sister got involved with someone... She was modelling for one of the big department stores at the time. *He* was one of their advertising executives—high flyer.' Aiden made a derisive sound in his throat. 'Against everyone's advice, she moved in with him. She was only twenty-one. Hell, she was just a baby.'

Kate's throat closed. 'This man—he was abusive?'

'Beat her up but only where it didn't show, of course.'

'That seems to be the pattern.'

'None of us had any idea,' Aiden went on. 'I for one, didn't particularly like the guy but then I'd decided it was Quinn's choice. I wish now I'd followed my instincts.'

Apprehension rushed at Kate. 'What happened?'

'She arrived at my apartment late one night. She had a black eye and a busted lip.'

'Oh, Aiden.' Kate went cold.

'I took her straight to Casualty for treatment, X-rays and so on.'

'And she was OK?'

'Eventually. I kept her with me until her face healed. She couldn't face Mum and Dad. But in the end they had to be told, of course. They were horrified but supportive, as they've always been with all of us. Quinn moved back home.'

'And the man?'

Aiden's mouth drew in. 'I wanted Quinn to press charges for assault but she was fearful of publicity. In the end she went to her boss who, thank heavens, took her seriously. It went to the

MD and after an internal investigation the cretin was "let go".'

'Without a reference, one would hope,' Kate said.

'I hope he found it very difficult to get another job at the same level. Quinn never heard anything from him or about him again.'

There was a long silence.

'How is Quinn now?' Kate asked quietly.

'She's great.' Aiden's mouth curved into a warm smile. 'She's married to a good guy and they have a fantastic little girl.'

'So it happened a while ago?'

'Yes, but it's something you don't forget.'

'No.' Kate could understand that. And it certainly explained his frustration with Leanne's outcome. 'Perhaps we need to have a chat about domestic violence at our next staff meeting. It's certainly out there and as doctors we need to refresh our strategies from time to time, don't you agree?'

Aiden lifted a shoulder. 'I guess it wouldn't

do any harm. Sorry I carried on a bit,' he added ruefully.

'Don't be. It's called sharing the load. In our profession, it's the only way to stay sane.' Kate flashed him a smile and he smiled back, looking relaxed at last. Kate was glad she'd had that effect on him. Very glad. 'I'll make the coffee. I think there's some chocolate mints somewhere as well.'

While the coffee filtered, they stacked the dishwasher together. 'Do you cook for yourself at home?' Kate asked.

'Mostly.' Aiden moved her gently out of the way to place the last of the plates in the dishwasher. 'I usually time things by the smoke alarm.'

'You don't!' Kate's eyes shot wide in disbelief. And then she smiled. Widely. 'Quite the joker, aren't you?'

With the coffee ready, Kate shook the chocolate mints onto a plate. 'Shall we take this through to the lounge?'

Aiden felt his heart pump a little. 'Let's just

stay here. The candle hasn't burned down yet.' And he could reach across the table and touch her. If he had a mind to.

They were halfway through their coffee when Aiden said quietly, 'Tell me about Cory.'

Well, that had come out of left field. Kate hesitated, her mind suddenly blank.

'That's if it's OK with you?'

Kate flicked him a guarded smile. 'It's fine.' But where to start? She took a steadying breath and began, 'I'd gone to the States to work. I'd lined up a job in Virginia, working in the ER at one of the university hospitals. Cory was a paramedic. One day he brought in a family who'd been overcome with smoke when their house had caught on fire. He was really concerned for the two little kids involved. He was coming off shift so he stuck around until they'd been given the all-clear. We had a coffee together. He teased me about my Aussie accent.' Kate smiled, as if the memory was sweet. 'Our relationship kind of went from there, I guess.'

A tiny pulse beat in Aiden's jaw as he took it all in. 'Was he always into extreme sports?'

'Pretty much. He taught me to climb.'

'How did you feel about that?'

Kate shrugged. 'I wanted to have a go. It was exhilarating but so physically demanding. Cory was a base jumper as well but I would never be into that.'

'That doesn't appeal to me either,' Aiden agreed. 'And the sky-diving?'

'It was his passion,' Kate said simply. 'He still kept it up even after we'd had the children. He always said it was safe. He knew what he was doing.' Kate was aware of holding herself very still. 'But there's always that one time when nature turns…'

'Oh, Kate.' Without warning, Aiden's hand reached out and covered hers. 'Would he have given it up if you'd asked him to?'

'I couldn't have done that.' Kate stared down at the hand covering hers. 'I would have felt as though I was taking something away that made him who he was.'

Aiden's eyes clouded and he thought, I'd chuck it in in a minute if I had a beautiful wife like Kate and a couple of kids to come home to.

'On the day of the accident, Cory was caught in a freak wind.' Now she'd started it seemed Kate couldn't stop.

'Certain weather conditions can trigger them,' Aiden responded quietly. 'It's every sky-diver's nightmare. Equivalent to being struck by lightning.'

Kate nodded. 'It literally caught him up and dropped him like a stone.'

'I'm so sorry, Kate.' Aiden squeezed her fingers and let them go.

Kate gave a brave little tilt to her head. 'It's been three years now. The kids and I have learned to live without him. You don't have a choice really. But I intend to make a good life for them. A happy life. Whatever it takes.'

'There's no question you're already doing that.' Aiden's gaze became shuttered. She was sitting so still, looking soft and so vulnerable, and with every male instinct in him he wanted to reach for her, wrap his strength around her. But right now he wasn't certain if she'd appreciate him doing that. Wasn't certain about her in any direction, for that matter. But he was certain of one thing. He'd better make himself scarce before he said something crazy, like suggesting they go to bed. His throat closed and he turned up his wrist to glance at his watch. 'Uh—I'd better go, let you get some sleep.' He gave a twisted half-smile. 'We're on deck again tomorrow.'

'Oh.' Kate blinked, as if coming out of a trance. 'Thanks for coming.'

'No, thank *you.* The meal was superb.'

Kate got to her feet. 'I'll walk you out.'

Halfway across the front veranda, Aiden stopped abruptly and turned. Lifting his hands, he placed them on Kate's shoulders, massaging them with a light, caressing touch. 'Goodnight, Kate.' Leaning forward, he placed a chaste kiss on her lips. 'Sleep well.'

With that, he moved away, taking the stairs quickly and walking out to the street. Kate stood motionless at the railings until his car had taken off. What an odd kind of evening it had turned out to be.

She turned and walked back inside, feeling an odd sense of something unfinished.

Halfway home, Aiden almost convinced himself to stop the car and turn back. He shouldn't have run out on Kate like that. God only knew what she must be thinking. But if he'd stayed…

If he'd stayed...

Oh, hell. He cringed at his ineptitude. But with Kate, everything felt different.

Kate slept fitfully and woke early. She lay still, looking at the ceiling and remembering how Aiden had cut and run. A brittle half-laugh jagged out of her throat. Obviously her baggage had scared the daylights out of him. But he'd asked about Cory. What was she supposed to have said? But had she given the impression she was still tied to her past? Perhaps that was it.

She groaned softly, pushing her head back into the pillow and covering her eyes with the backs of her hands, realising she wanted a thousand repeat performances of how they'd kissed in the surgery that day.

And more.

When her mobile rang beside her on the night table, she had one immediate thought—Aiden. She picked up the phone, eagerness lighting her voice. 'Kate speaking.'

'Oh, darling, I'm sorry to ring so early.'

'Mum!' Kate shot upright. 'Is something wrong? Is it the kids?'

'Well—it's Mia, actually.'

'Is she ill?' Kate's voice held a thread of panic. Her precious little girl had been born nine weeks premature. The anguish Kate had felt back then for the fragile state of her baby still surfaced when she least expected it.

'No, not ill, but she was weepy last night and didn't want to go to bed. Dad read to her for ages and she finally dropped off. But she woke screaming just a while ago and, frankly, Kate, I think she needs you.'

'I'm on my way.' Kate threw her legs over the side of the bed.

'What about your work?'

'Mum, it's not my regular job. It's the after-hours clinic. They can get someone else to fill in.'

'And if they can't?'

'Then the backlog of patients can go to the casualty department at the hospital.'

'I'm sorry to worry you, darling,' Kate's mother apologised again.'

'Mum, you did exactly the right thing. My kids will always come first. You know that. Tell Mia I'm on my way, will you, please?'

'I'll do that. We'll be so pleased to see you.'

Kate threw the phone down. She looked blindly around for a second and then pulled on jeans and a T-shirt, stuffed her feet into her canvas shoes and made a quick call to the bathroom. Five minutes later, she was reversing her car out of the garage.

As she drove, Kate decided she'd spend the day at the farm. She deserved a break. And she could lend a hand. She chewed on her bottom lip. Perhaps the care of her children was getting too much for her parents. Even though they loved their grandchildren, Kate knew they were full on. Busy and demanding. She'd talk to Mum about it.

Aiden stuck his head out of his consulting room and craned his neck up and down the corridor for the umpteenth time. He hadn't seen Kate that morning. Perhaps she'd been unusually busy. Still… Closing his office door, he strode along to reception. Rosie looked up. 'Aiden?'

'Hi, Rosie.' He planted his hands on the counter top and leaned forward confidentially. 'I haven't seen Kate this morning.'

'She had to cancel,' Rosie said. 'Family matter. Dr Charlton's here if you wanted to consult about something.'

'No.' Aiden held up a disclaiming hand. 'It's fine.'

'Not so busy so far.' Rosie smiled.

'Let's hope it continues.' Aiden made his way back to his office. Throwing himself into his chair, he wondered about Kate. A family matter. That could mean anything. He picked up the phone. He'd call her on her mobile. But before he could activate the number, a tiny speck of caution prevailed. He put the phone back in its cradle. He had no claim on Kate Preston. Unless and until she gave him that privilege.

'It's lovely here, isn't it, Mum?' Kate said. They'd taken the children for a paddle in the little creek that bordered the farm's boundary and now they were sitting against a leopard tree in the dappled shade.

Gillian Morris looked closely at her daughter. 'I'm glad you've enjoyed your break today. I think you needed it.'

'Probably.' Kate looked thoughtful. 'Are the kids getting too much for you and Dad? Perhaps I should try to organise some home help.'

'Darling, don't get things out of proportion. It was a glitch with Mia, that's all. And now it's sorted out.'

'Yes, it seems to be.' Kate looked indulgently across to where Luke and Mia were sailing the little boats their grandfather had made for them on his wood lathe. They seemed happy and content. And yet… 'Do you think they miss Cory?'

Gillian thought for a minute. 'Not specifically, but perhaps they just miss having a dad.'

Her mother's words stayed with Kate all the way home from the farm and into the next morning as she drove to work. Luke and Mia probably *did* need a dad but it wasn't as though she could walk into a shop and buy one!

With mixed thoughts, Kate turned her car into the parking lot at the surgery.

She was early by design. She needed time to gather herself before she spoke to Aiden. She should have called him yesterday, shown the courtesy of letting him know she wouldn't be in. But, then, he could have called her, she reasoned. The fact that he hadn't only reinforced her belief that he'd backed away.

In her consulting room, she stowed her medical case and then decided she'd make a coffee and try to catch up on some reading. These days medical information seemed to change almost every other day.

As she made her way along the corridor to the staffroom, she thought how quiet it was. Well, that was understandable. She was obviously the only person here.

Pushing open the door, she came to a dead stop. 'Oh—Aiden!' She swallowed dryly, her heart swooping out of rhythm. 'I had no idea you were in. Your car wasn't in its usual place.'

'Hi….' His gaze ran over her quickly. She seemed fine. He couldn't believe the relief he felt. 'My wheels are in for a service. I walked from the garage. How are you?'

'I'm fine, thanks.' She brought the jug back to the boil and spooned coffee into a mug. 'Sorry about yesterday. I meant to call.'

'I meant to call *you*.'

'Did you?' Kate brought her gaze up expectantly.

'Mmm.' He rubbed a hand around the back of his neck. 'I wanted to. I just didn't know whether you'd welcome it.'

Why would he think that? She turned away to get milk from the fridge. 'Mia had a bit of a meltdown. I had to go out to the farm.'

'But she's OK now?'

'Just needed her mum. My parents came back with us last night. They'll drop the kids at school. That gave me a window to come in early.'

'That's good.' Aiden nodded. 'I think you do an amazing job combining work and family. I know it can't be easy but you do it so well.'

Kate felt her face warm at his praise. He seemed to care about her and her children. Really care. Yet that wasn't the impression he'd left behind on Saturday when he'd left so abruptly. 'Why did you think I'd not welcome a call from you yesterday?'

He lifted a shoulder, his mouth working for a moment. 'Our wires got a bit crossed when I left your place on Saturday night.'

Kate took her time returning the milk to the fridge. Suddenly her nerve ends were tingling, her breathing uncomfortably tight. 'Yes, I guess they did.' She lifted her head, searing her gaze with his.

In the complexity of the silence that followed, Aiden didn't stop to analyse his thoughts. He only knew that here he was with Kate. And they were alone.

Throwing caution to the winds, he stepped closer.

'Kate...?' He reached out, sliding the tips of his fingers over her cheek, feeling the gentle throb of heat under her skin, the feminine, fragile line of her jaw. Even as his thumb lifted her chin, his fingers were seeking her nape, drawing her to him.

He lowered his head slowly, giving her the chance to break away if that's what she wanted. But she didn't, her lips giving a tiny sigh of welcome as his mouth touched hers, settling over its softness, savouring the contact with light, lingering sips, feeling their instant response and teasing them into a more open kiss.

Kate needed this. Oh, how she needed this. In seconds they were taking what they wanted from each other, turning the kiss into a wild sensual dance.

Power kicked through Aiden. He had to win this woman, make her his. The challenge ignited him into gathering her closer. Oh, God, this was so good. And he wanted more. His hand found a sure path as it slid under her jacket and smoothed the soft cotton of her shirt where her waist curved into her hip.

Kate was drowning in feelings she hadn't experienced for the longest time. It felt right. Pure. And when his hand encircled her breast, she moaned at the sweet intimacy, wanting it never to end. Being with him like this felt so good, wonderful, drugging her senses until she was liquid in his arms.

But this was their place of work.

Kate wrenched her mouth away, stepping back. Her chest heaving, her pulse racing. 'Aiden…we have to stop.'

'No…' His voice was rough edged, husky. He took a step towards her.

'Yes.' The look of naked desire in his gaze

called to her but she held up her hands. 'In a few minutes the place will be swarming. We can't do this here.'

'Where, then?' He swung away, locking his hands on top of his head in a movement of frustration. 'When?'

Kate took a deep, shuddering breath. 'I need to think.' She shook her head, adding carefully, '*We* need to think.'

He bit out an expletive. 'This is killing us, Kate!'

Kate was aware of holding herself very still. 'I'm not a free agent, Aiden. I can't make snap decisions about something like this, no matter how much I'd love to.'

Their eyes met and suddenly the atmosphere was charged again.

'Oh, Kate...' His voice caught and his gaze flickered all the way down her body and back up again. 'I'm sorry. I'm just being totally selfish.'

Or totally male. Kate took refuge in a shaky smile. 'I guess we'll work something out.'

Suddenly they turned as one, hearing the echoing footsteps along the corridor, a murmur of voices, the opening and closing of doors.

'Next Saturday,' Aiden said, his voice low and urgent. 'Come to my place. Bring the kids. Stay the weekend—please.'

Kate felt her heart go into free-fall, her throat as dry as dust, the sweet sting of anticipation already slithering up her spine. Picking up her cooling coffee, she moved to the door and opened it slightly. She looked back at him. 'I'll try,' she said throatily. It took all her willpower to leave him and go back to her consulting room.

By the time Kate had dealt with a very busy morning surgery, she had almost regained her calm. The morning had flown and that was probably a good thing, she decided, walking out to Reception to call in Ashleigh Callea, her last patient before they closed the surgery for lunch.

'Come in, Ashleigh.' Kate smiled. 'Take a seat.'

'Thanks.' The young woman dropped into the chair, hunching forward, a water bottle clasped in her hands. 'I'm pregnant,' she said, flatly. 'And I feel so ill.'

'It's probably morning sickness.' Kate gave a wry smile. 'And I'm afraid it goes with the territory. How far along are you?'

'Five weeks or so. The minute I get out of bed, I want to throw up—and I usually do,' she added with a grimace. 'God, it's awful…' Tears clumped on the young woman's lashes and she swiped them away. 'I need to keep my job but it's such an effort. We've just bought a house and we're trying to service a mortgage. I didn't mean to get pregnant so soon.'

'But it happens.' Kate commiserated. 'So, how can I help you today?'

Ashleigh's shoulders lifted in a defeated sigh. 'Can you tell me why I'm so ill? And how long it's going to go on for? And what can I do to feel half-normal again?'

'Have you eaten anything this morning?' Kate leaned forward and slipped the blood-pressure cuff around her patient's arm.

'Couldn't.'

'Your BP's OK,' Kate said as she took the reading. 'So first things first. Let's see what we can do about making life more bearable for you.' Picking up the phone, she pressed the key that would connect her with Reception. 'Oh, hi, Vic. Could you be an angel and bring in a pot of tea and some crackers, please?'

'Right away, Kate,' Vicky responded cheerfully, as though the request was an everyday occurrence.

'Surely you don't do this for all your patients?' Ashleigh placed her bottle of water on the edge of the desk and wrapped her arms tightly across her tummy.

'Only the special ones.' Kate twinkled a smile. 'Besides, we can't have you leaving feeling worse than when you came in, can we? And for the record, I do know exactly how you're feeling.'

'Well, it's more than my husband does.' Ashleigh closed her eyes and bit her lips together.

'Do you have family here?' Kate asked, hoping to build a background for her patient, and if she managed to get Ashleigh talking, perhaps it might take her mind temporarily off her negative feelings.

Ashleigh shook her head. 'Michael and I came for a drive one weekend and just loved the town. Oddly enough, the council were recruiting and we both landed jobs. Michael is a carpenter and I work in the council offices. Our extended families live in Brisbane.'

Vicki arrived promptly with the tea and crackers.

'Oh, this is heaven,' Ashleigh sighed a few minutes later, wrapping her hands around the tea mug and taking long mouthfuls of the reviving brew.

Kate ran a professional eye over her patient. She was regaining some colour. 'Try to nibble a cracker as well,' she encouraged. 'It will help combat the nausea.'

'This would never happen in a city practice.' Ashleigh gave a wobbly smile.

Kate leaned back in her chair. 'Well, we tend to take a bit more time here. Feeling better?'

'Mmm. Thank you so much for this, Dr Preston.' Ashleigh blinked rapidly. 'But can you explain to me why I'm feeling so grotty?'

'Strange as it may seem, pregnancy nausea is one of nature's clever ways to maintain the expectant mother's health,' Kate said. 'The simple reasoning is, if you're feeling sick then you're inclined not to eat anything that could cause you to develop a tummy bug that could in turn harm the foetus.'

Ashleigh nodded. 'Makes sense. I could almost put up with it now I know that.'

'Are you feeling extra-tired at the moment?'

'Oh, lord, yes! I could sleep and sleep. Is that part of it?'

'Don't be disheartened,' Kate said kindly. 'The intense feeling of fatigue will pass eventually. And if you think about what your body is trying to achieve—manufacture a baby and a placenta, as well as whatever's necessary for the mother's body—you can understand why you're so tired at the moment.'

'How long will it last?'

'Well, it's all about the body's hormonal changes,' Kate said. 'But usually it settles down by about the twelfth to sixteenth week of pregnancy.'

Ashleigh frowned. 'I can't afford to be so unwell that I can't do my job, though.'

'No. So it's important to have regular, small, light meals. As soon as you feel hungry, eat.'

'But not take-away?'

'Probably not a good idea at the moment. Anything with excessive sugar is a no-no as well. I'll give you a list of suitable foods. Get your husband to bring you a cup of tea and dry toast or some crackers first thing in the morning before you get up. That will help enormously. But take it easy. Remember big changes are taking place in your body. Taking vitamin B6 can be beneficial as well.'

Ashleigh had listened intently. She brightened. 'I feel much more hopeful now. I can pack little snacks to take to work.'

'And keep up your fluids,' Kate said. 'And get out in the fresh air at lunchtime. That will all help you to feel better able to cope. Oh.' Kate flapped a hand. 'Stay away from strong odours if you can.'

Ashleigh managed a chuckle. 'Looks like Michael will have to take over cleaning the bathroom, then.'

'Excellent idea.' Kate joined in the chuckle and then she sobered. 'Now, Ashleigh, I want you to promise me that if you're still feeling unwell in, say, another week or ten days, unable to keep your food down, then come back and see me. There are things we'll need to do to get you over the hump of the first trimester.'

'Hospital?'

'Perhaps. It stands to reason if you're continuing to vomit, you're going to dehydrate. That's no good for either you or your baby. But I'm sure if you can manage to eat your light meals and get plenty of rest, you'll be fine. Are you intending to have your baby here?

'Oh, yes, absolutely. Can I keep coming to see you for that?'

'For the early months, yes.' Kate dug through

her leaflets and placed several in front of her patient. 'As your pregnancy progresses, we hand you over to the midwifery department at the hospital. They'll monitor you and support you for the delivery of your baby. It's called shared care. It works very well.' Kate smiled. 'And I believe they've recently had a birthing suite installed. I haven't seen it yet but I hear from a friend that it's lovely.' It had Jo's approval so that was enough recommendation for Kate.

Ashleigh picked up the leaflets and scanned them. 'It's all going to happen, isn't it?' She looked at Kate in slight awe. 'I'll be a mum.'

'There's no feeling quite like it.' Kate smiled softly, thinking of her own experience. 'Now, do you feel well enough to pop on the scales for me? We'll get a file going for you.'

'Mmm. I can do that.' There was a new lightness in Ashleigh's bearing as she stood obligingly and went across to stand on the scales.

CHAPTER SEVEN

KATE felt drained by the end of the day which was about to extend even further, she lamented. She had to attend the rescheduled staff meeting. Getting up from her desk, she stretched, working her shoulders as she walked across to the window and peered out. She sighed. On glorious, big-sky days like this, she wished she was outdoors. She needed to see the setting sun gild the tops of the mountains, turning their outlines into purple shapes of mystery and leave the sky shot with brazen stripes of orange and gold.

Oh, please. She turned, shaking herself out of her fanciful thoughts, when the knock sounded on her door and Aiden poked his head in. He gave a crooked, slightly uncertain smile that tipped her heart off kilter. 'OK to come in?'

'Of course.' She looked at him a little warily.

She hoped he wasn't going to pressure her about next weekend.

'I haven't seen you all day,' he said mournfully.

Kate shrugged. 'Wall-to-wall appointments. You?'

'Same.' He moved across to her desk, hooking his thigh over the corner. 'Can I do anything for you?' He gave her a funny little smile that made her heart turn over again.

Kate raised a brow. 'Like what?' She moved back to her desk so she was quite close to him.

He smiled again. 'Hug, maybe? Massage—Oops! Probably not that. Not here.'

Kate gave a strangled laugh. 'A coffee that was actually hot might be nice.'

'Done.' He slipped off her desk and straightened. 'I might even manage to pinch some of that almond shortbread Vicki keeps hidden.'

'Yum...' Kate licked her lips, stopping abruptly when she saw his eyes darken.

'Ah...Katie...' he whispered, his breath hissing out, elongating the sound. 'I've missed you every second of today.' He reached out, touching her cheek.

Kate swallowed roughly. His mouth was just a breath away. Just a breath…

A beat of stillness.

The kiss when it finally came brought a long shuddering sigh from her chest and she could feel his hand trembling against her cheek.

'You're an angel,' he whispered. 'And I want you.'

Kate heard a whimper of longing—her own? Her body called to his, finding a home against its solid muscularity.

His hand cupped her breast and she arched into his palm, aching for him, for the weight of him poised over her until the moment she became flesh of his flesh, part of him. Inseparable.

On a harsh breath, Aiden pulled back, hauling himself under control. He gave her a resigned look. 'Let's get that coffee.'

'Sorry to hold you back, people,' Angelo apologised. 'We'll whip through as quickly as we can.'

Matters relating to the running of the surgery were dealt with expeditiously and then Angelo said, 'Anyone have any patient concerns they'd like to pass along?'

There were negative murmurs and then Aiden spoke up. 'I had a patient at the after-hours clinic on Saturday. I thought I'd handled it sensitively enough to get a good result for her but the outcome proved otherwise. I've spoken to Kate about it.' He looked at his male colleagues. 'I'd value your input.'

Brady sat back and folded his arms across his chest. 'Better run it by us, then, mate.'

Aiden told his story, quickly and precisely.

'I can empathise with your frustration,' Brady said.

'I felt like punching walls,' Aiden admitted wryly. 'Instead I held it together and gave Leanne the address of the local women's shelter. I told her to go there if she had trouble in future.' He shrugged. 'Maybe she will, maybe she won't.'

'Perhaps you should have directed her there in the first place,' Angelo said.

'I was thinking of her boy. I figured if she had a chance to reconnect with him, it might have just tipped the balance and got her away.'

'The issues surrounding domestic violence are complex,' Kate contributed quietly. 'According to the latest stats, fifty per cent of people would rather turn a blind eye than interfere. So I'd say your initiatives were fine, Aiden. It was Leanne's choice not to follow through.'

Aiden sent her a grateful look. 'I wondered later why she took the trouble to come into the clinic instead of going to Casualty. Busy department, chances are she could have been in and out with no questions asked.'

'But if she presented at Casualty, she'd have had a longer wait to be seen,' Kate said practically. 'Fliss O'Byrne said the place was heaving. There were lots of pickers in with start-of-season ills. Leanne obviously weighed up her chances of being recognised by someone from the caravan park. She wouldn't want Wayne finding out from another source that she'd sought medical attention. When she was ready to tell him, she'd have a plausible story to cover herself. From what I've observed, women in abusive relationships learn pretty quickly they need strategies to keep the peace at home.'

'Now that I think about it, she'd left it to the last minute to present at the clinic,' Aiden said thoughtfully. 'And she was running scared.'

'I think Kate is spot on,' Brady said.

'I've struck a few cases of domestic abuse in my time,' Angelo said measuredly. 'Sad to say, many women, and it's mostly women who are the victims, don't consider an abusive partner is violent. *It's just how he is.*'

Brady frowned. 'You said they're pickers, Aiden. How is your patient going to work with a bunged-up hand?'

'Oh, she'll work,' Aiden growled. 'In case Wayne beats her up if she doesn't. He probably confiscates her pay.'

Kate shuddered. No wonder Aiden had been upset by the result of all his efforts to get the woman away. Most men saw their role as protectors. She knew instinctively Aiden would be one of those.

'Well, this has been a good wake-up call for all of us.' Angelo began to wind up the meeting. 'Domestic violence is a reality unfortunately. If your patient presents to any of us in future, Aiden, we'll certainly have background. Thank you.'

'I just wish I could have got Leanne away.'

Brady snorted. 'And I daresay all of us would like to come up with a lasting cure for cancer. You did well, mate,' he said to his colleague. 'And you don't know for certain she won't take your advice and skip town eventually.'

Kate and Aiden left the surgery together. 'Are the kids in after-school care today?' Aiden turned aside to flick the remote on his newly serviced four-wheel-drive.

Kate nodded. 'I'm on my way to collect them now.'

'Would it be OK if I called round later and said hello to them?'

She glanced away, but not before he'd seen the uncertainty in her eyes. 'I…guess it would be all right.'

'Kate…' He lifted a hand and brought her gaze back to meet his, his look reproachful. 'I don't have an ulterior motive. I'd really like to get to know Luke and Mia.'

Of course he would, she thought guiltily. If he wanted their relationship to have any chance, he had to form a bond with her children. She understood that. And if she wanted it as well, she'd have to meet him halfway. 'Sorry.' She drummed up a smile. 'Stay for dinner if you like. Mum said she'd left a cottage pie for us.'

He looked at his watch. 'I have a squash date at the sports centre in about ten minutes. Perhaps you and I could eat later? I'll bring some Thai. What do you like?'

'Anything's fine. If you're sure? It's Monday, the kids might be a bit ratty.'

Aiden frowned. Was she trying to put up road-blocks? Surely not. If they wanted to find out whether this thing between them had any substance, they couldn't baulk at the first hurdle. 'Kate, I like kids. Hell, I'm Uncle Aiden to five of them.'

Kate looked up into his eyes, saw the signs of strain around them and felt the need to explain. 'This is all new territory for me, Aiden,' she said quietly. 'And this—us—has happened so fast.'

'I agree. But I also think you're putting too much pressure on yourself.'

Kate gave a soft, wry little groan. 'I'm getting way too heavy again, aren't I?'

'Oh, I don't know.' He ran a blatant appraisal over her from head to toe. 'I'd say you're just about perfect.'

She mock-swiped him with her car keys. 'See you when we see you, then. Have a good game.'

When Kate told the children Aiden was calling round, Mia was bubbling with excitement, Luke was more circumspect. 'Why is he coming?'

'Well, just to be friendly,' Kate said, trying to keep everything low key. 'And to keep me company for a while. You have friends at school but I don't have many grown-up friends here yet.'

'I like Aiden,' Mia said later, finishing off a drawing for their visitor. She looked at her mother. 'Does Aiden have a little girl like me?'

'No, honey. He doesn't have children.'

Luke and Mia were fed, bathed and in their pyjamas when Aiden finally arrived. Mia trotted beside Kate when she went to answer the door.

'I made you a drawing,' Mia piped up before Aiden had one foot in the door.

'Did you?' He faked surprise and smiled down at the child. 'I can't wait to see it.' He handed Kate the bag of take-away food. 'Can you keep this hot for a while?'

'Of course I can. Thank you.'

He winked. 'My pleasure.'

Kate gave a guarded smile, her heartbeat quickening. And she thought all over again how natural he seemed with her child as he let himself be tugged along by a small insistent hand.

Entering the lounge room, Aiden took in the scene quickly. Uh-oh. Luke was wearing defensiveness like a cloak. No doubt seeing himself as the man of the house. In his own childish way riding shotgun over his family. Hellish for a little kid to feel he had such responsibility. Aiden shook his head, feeling a new dimension of uncertainty for the situation he found himself in. But he'd known all along Kate and her children came as a package. He'd *known*. 'Hey, Luke,' he said casually.

'Hey…' Luke looked up warily from the puzzle he was working on.

'How are things?' Aiden sat next to the boy on the sofa.

'OK.'

'Here's my drawing.' Mia thrust the A4 sheet of paper on to Aiden's lap. 'This is Mummy and me and Luke. We're having a picnic.'

'Yes, I can see that,' Aiden said diplomatically, looking at the stick figures so carefully drawn.

'Mummy's the one with the long hair,' Mia explained seriously.

'Uh-huh. Mummy is very pretty.' Aiden turned to the small girl pressed against his knee. 'I'll

take this home and put it on my fridge, shall I?'
Heck. Between the two Preston women he felt caught in a honey trap. Not that he wanted out. Far from it. He looked up as Kate came in, patting the space next to him.

A bit reluctantly, Kate joined him on the sofa, trying to disguise the sudden leap in her pulse when his thigh brushed against hers. 'How was your squash game?' she asked, noticing his hair was still damp and spiky from the shower.

'Good.' His teeth flashed in a white grin. 'I won.'

Of course he did. Kate raised a brow. She guessed he won at most things he tackled. 'Luke has a new soccer game,' she said, wanting to draw her little boy into the circle. 'I'm not much competition but you might like the challenge.'

'You bet.' Aiden caught on immediately. 'Like a hand to set it up, Luke?'

Luke shook his head. 'I can do it myself.'

Of course Aiden let Luke win. And amid promises of a rematch some time soon, Kate persuaded the children it was time for bed.

'Help yourself to a drink,' she told Aiden. 'I won't be long.'

Aiden went through to the kitchen. He poured a glass of orange juice from a carton in the fridge and began to drink it slowly, thoughtfully. 'All set?' he asked when Kate reappeared.

'Out like lights. Mia didn't even want a story. You'll have to come round more often.'

Ah. Vaguely disconcerted, Aiden swiftly finished the rest of his drink.

'I'll dish up the food,' Kate said. 'You must be starved.'

'I got a beef curry.'

'It smells delicious.' Kate set out the platters of curry, steamed vegetables and rice. 'Bowls there on the shelf behind you. Don't stand on ceremony.' She turned away to get a jug of water and glasses and brought them to the table.

They began dipping into their food, eating hungrily. 'You've no idea how much you've lightened my parental load this evening,' Kate said, scooping more rice into her bowl.

'Luke seemed a bit put out by my being here.

I didn't expect it.' Aiden's admission came with a slight frown. 'Yet when I played football with him at the park, he was quite accepting of my company.'

'That's because it was neutral territory,' Kate explained. 'Tonight you're here in his home. He feels a bit uncertain.'

'How hard is it to be a good parent?'

Kate looked across the table at him. He seemed very serious. 'Well, normally, you're with your children from the moment they're born. The skills more or less grow as they grow. But it stands to reason some kids are easier to handle than others.'

'Luke and Mia are quite different in temperament, aren't they?'

'Mia is very tactile,' Kate agreed. 'Whereas Luke keeps his distance until he's sure about things and people.'

'It's a huge responsibility, isn't it? Bringing up kids.' And bringing up someone else's was fraught with pitfalls. What if he messed it up. Messed *them* up?

Kate came in quietly, 'So, are we having some kind of reality check here?'

Aiden gave a huff of denial. 'It just bears thinking about, that's all.'

'You told me earlier I was placing too much pressure on myself. Perhaps you're guilty of doing the same thing. There's no actual rush, is there?'

Aiden looked down at his food, seeming to lose his appetite. 'This, us, your kids—it's all pretty new for me, Kate.'

Kate swallowed the lump in her throat. 'It's new for me too—having a man in my life again.'

He sighed and rubbed the back of his neck as though to relieve a kink. 'I realise that. I don't know how we got onto this point anyway.'

'Because it's important,' Kate returned a little shakily. 'And we should talk about it.'

'But not let it weigh us down?' He blinked for a second and his mouth lifted in a dry twist. 'Could I interest you in a hug, Dr Preston?'

'Oh, yes, please…'

They stood as one, their bodies flowing almost in slow motion towards each other until they met.

Aiden held her to him. Reaching back, he released her hair from its knot so that it streamed over her shoulders. Then he brought his hands across her collarbone and down to cup her breasts almost reverently. 'Oh, sweet…' he said softly. 'When are you coming home with me?'

'Whenever you like…' she murmured on a little sigh, feeling an overload of the sexual tension that had been building between them heighten even further.

'We need to make plans, then.' His arms made two strong bands of warmth across her back. 'Proper plans. Because this has to be right for you—and your children.'

'Thank you for understanding.'

'Can you do next weekend at my place, then?' Aiden asked.

Kate hesitated. 'I can't ask my parents to have the kids again so soon. They're quite a handful.'

'Bring them along. I thought I'd made that clear.'

She nodded. He had. 'If you're sure?'

Aiden sensed her uncertainty. 'If you're worried about privacy, don't be. No offence, Kate, but this place is a dolls' house compared to mine. It's huge and the master bedroom is quite separate from the rest of the house and the windows look out on to the mountains. It's amazingly peaceful, secluded.' His eyes darkened and his voice lowered. 'Just made for lovers.'

And how many had he had there? Kate felt a twist of jealousy. But she couldn't think like that. It was ridiculous to think he'd spent his whole life waiting for *her*. 'Are you very rich, then?'

He snorted. 'After paying my way through medical school? Unlikely. But I had the chance to buy the acreage at a good price. And my dad's a builder. We laid a concrete slab and worked out a plan for a ranch-style dwelling. Not difficult when you know what you're doing. The whole family helped with the inside painting. Mum threw in some furniture she'd inherited from my grandmother which she'd had in storage because the girls didn't care for it. But I was glad to have it. The only thing I wanted complete autonomy about was the master suite. I wanted space. And a view.'

'And it seems you've got both.'

He slid her a hopeful glance. 'So, you'll come and visit for the weekend, then?'

Kate felt her unease melt away. 'It sounds wonderful.'

CHAPTER EIGHT

NEXT morning, Kate whizzed through her appointments on a new high. She glanced at her watch; only half an hour until lunch and for once she had a few minutes to call her own.

A soft smile curved her mouth and she thought of the coming weekend. And Aiden. When Vicky buzzed her, she picked up the phone. 'Kate, could you see one tiny patient? Her mum's just brought her in. They're from the caravan park.'

'Is it an emergency?' Kate asked. 'If so she'd be better off to go straight to Casualty.'

'Doesn't appear to be.' Vicky's voice lowered. 'Nappy rash from what I gather. The bub is six months old. New-mum panic probably.'

'Well, I imagine you and I have both been

there,' Kate said wryly. 'OK, I'll see her. Do we have a name?'

'Lily Anderson, Mum is Melanie.'

'Right. Just give me five, Vic.' Kate thought for a moment. In the treatment of rashes, she'd been there and done that. She did know of something that could help. Jo would probably know if the product was available in Mt Pryde. It was worth a call.

'Come in, Melanie.' Kate welcomed the young mother in and introduced herself. 'I gather you're concerned about your baby's nappy rash.'

'It seems to have gotten worse overnight.' Melanie bit her lip. 'I don't know whether I've done something wrong or—'

'Oh, I wouldn't think you have,' Kate reassured quickly. 'In any case, most nappy rashes are a normal part of babyhood. It's not a sign of neglect on the part of the parent.'

'Oh, that's such a relief!' Melanie held the infant to her. 'She's been doing so well otherwise.'

Kate smiled. 'Just pop Lily over here on the bed and let's have a look, shall we?'

As soon as her nappy was removed, the little one began kicking happily, her bright gaze darting everywhere like a small bird's. Kate's look became soft. Apart from the red areas of skin around her bottom, Lily looked healthy and well-cared for. 'How long would you say, Lily has had the rash?' Kate asked.

'A few days but then as I said, it just seems to have gotten worse not better.'

'Any changes in her care that would account for it?'

'None at all. I follow the same routine. Except—the water at the caravan park is hard. Won't soap easily.'

'So, you might be using a bit more soap?' Kate wondered.

'I try not to, but maybe…'

Kate nodded, satisfied. 'Her nappy doesn't appear wet, Melanie, so pop it back on and then we'll have a chat.'

When the young mother was seated, Kate said, 'There are a couple of things you can do that should make Lily more comfortable. Don't use the commercial baby-wipes, they're inclined to dry the skin. And I'll give you the name of a cream you can buy over the counter at the chemist, that should bring rapid results. In the meantime, you can try using a natural soap made from goat's milk. It's wonderfully soft and I've personal experience of it working really well on rashes of any kind and in really hard water.'

Melanie's eyes widened. 'I've never heard of that. Would I be able to get it here?'

'Yes. I've just checked and it seems the members of the Country Women's Association market their various arts and crafts at a little shop next to the library.'

'The CWA shop?' Melanie nodded eagerly. 'I've been in there. They have all kinds of really great stuff.'

'And apparently one of their members has a goat herd,' Kate added. 'And she's learned the art of soap-making. It's an excellent product from what I hear.'

'Oh, that'll be such a help. Thanks so much, Dr Preston.'

'So, how is it living at the caravan park?' Kate asked.

'Well, we're just there for picking season. This is our fourth year here. But I'm not picking this year on account of the baby. But my husband, James, is working pretty long hours. The money is good and he works for a nice family. Even so,' Melanie considered, placing a soft kiss on her baby's head, 'we've talked about settling somewhere now we have Lily.'

Kate listened intently. 'Where would you like to settle?'

'Not sure. We'd need permanent jobs and neither of us is trained for anything. Well, James did two years nurse training but we wanted to travel a bit and we've managed to see a lot of Australia picking. But as I said, it's probably time to set down some roots for Lily. And we've always loved coming here to Mt Pryde,' Melanie said wistfully. 'But I doubt there'd be permanent jobs here.'

'Perhaps your husband could reconsider nursing,' Kate said helpfully.

Melanie looked doubtful. 'We've talked about it, but he'd have to go back to uni and that would mean living in a city again. Neither of us is keen on that.'

Kate thought for a moment. 'Would he consider becoming a paramedic? With his nursing experience, he'd be a likely candidate.'

'We've never thought of that…' Melanie seemed impressed. 'And he liked nursing so I guess he'd be quite tuned in to another medically-related job. Would they have any vacancies here, do you think?'

'Only one way to find out,' Kate smiled. 'Give their headquarters a call or pop in and see someone. They may have an application form James could fill in.'

'That'd be magic!' Melanie's eyes shone. 'We could rent a little house and I'd get work.'

'Of course you would.' Kate looked at the eager young woman in front of her and the now-sleeping infant. 'And Mt Pryde seems a very good town for new beginnings. I hope it works out for you, Melanie.'

'Thanks,' Melanie smiled, juggling the baby across to her other arm. 'I hope so too.'

'I'll walk out with you,' Kate said.'Do you have a pram?'

'I left it in reception.' Melanie made a small face. 'I had a bit of trouble getting it through the front door.'

'I'll give you a hand then.' Perhaps they should re-think the design of the doors to make it easier for parents with prams, Kate considered. She'd bring it up at the next team meeting.

Kate held the door open while Melanie manipulated her pram through and then watched as the young mother set off across the forecourt, her step eager as she went about her business. Kate looked thoughtful as she closed the door. She very much hoped the little family would be able to settle in Mt Pryde and carve out a happy life.

'Kate, phone.' Vicky waggled the hand-piece aloft. 'Your mum. I'll put it through to your room.'

Kate turned, finger-waving her thanks and returned to her office.

'Hi, Mum,' Kate said brightly. 'This is a nice surprise.'

'Is it all right to ring you at the surgery?'

'Of course it is.' Kate heard the hesitation in her mother's voice. 'If I'm with a patient, Vicky will let me know and I'll return your call as soon as I'm free.'

'Oh, that's good, love. I just remembered I hadn't let you know about our Hay Festival next Saturday. I promised Luke and Mia we'd take them. It's always such fun,' Gillian went on happily. 'Folk have fashioned some wonderful hay sculptures all over the township and there'll be the usual stalls and things. And I believe they're having a demonstration of miniature models, trains and tractors and so on. Luke would find that interesting. Dad could take him along to that. And there's a fashion parade of children's clothes that you and Mia would love.'

'Saturday, you said, Mum?' Kate's fingers tightened on the phone. Saturday was promised to Aiden. She couldn't let him down. She just couldn't. But then Mum sounded as excited as a girl, so happy these days to have her grandchildren nearby. Now I know what it means to be between a rock and hard place, Kate groaned silently.

'I'll be helping on the CWA stall,' Gillian came in chattily. 'I've done heaps of my lavender sachets. The blooms were very good this year. You'll need to come early, darling. Oh, and stay the night, hmm? That way you won't have the drive home and the kids will be tired.'

Oh, help. Kate clamped on her bottom lip. She should be placing Aiden first here. She wanted to. But the happy, hopeful note in her mother's voice tugged at her heartstrings. Her parents did so much for her, she couldn't disappoint them.

Aiden would just have to understand.

Almost as if she'd conjured him up, he rapped and came in, as Kate put the phone down. 'Hey,' he said softly, closing the door and walking over to her desk. 'Coming to lunch? Fantastic smell coming from the staff room. Penny must have sent in one of her hot pots. And I'm starved.' He held out his hand and Kate took it and stood to her feet. 'I thought about you the moment I woke this morning.' He lifted their clasped hands and held her knuckles to his mouth. 'Did you think about me?'

Kate felt her heart contract. She knew without the shadow of a doubt she'd fallen in love with him. Madly. Deeply. She managed a wry smile. 'I'm sure I would have but Mia jumped all over me first thing.' Lifting her other hand, she stroked the faint cleft in his chin. 'But you've definitely been in my thoughts today.'

His look was soft and he squeezed her fingers gently. 'It's all starting to come together for us, isn't it?'

A tiny frown of uncertainty marked Kate's forehead. He had every right to think that. Now, she was going to have to gut him. 'Aiden…' She drew the seam of her lips together. 'I have something to tell you that's going to scuttle our plans for the weekend. I'm sorry but there's not a lot I can do about it.'

'Is someone ill?'

'No, nothing like that,' Kate was quick to reassure him. 'But Mum just called me.' She went on then to outline the plans her mother had made for her and the children.

Aiden released her hand and parked himself on the edge of her desk. He folded his arms and seemed to be thinking. 'Where do your parents live?'

'Out at Lakeview.'

'OK… That's not so far from my place, actually,' he said slowly. 'Give or take a few back roads. Why don't I tag along, yeah?' he smiled at her waiting for her answer.

'Oh—' Kate felt almost paralysed by the look of sheer expectation in his face. 'Would you *want* to do that?' She returned his question with one of her own.

'Oh, Kate, sweet Kate.' He shook his head at her. 'When are you going to realise this is serious business between us? I want to be with you, no matter where.'

'But it's a hay festival! Won't you be bored?'

'No.' He slid off the desk and looked down

at her. 'Not for a second. And it will give me a chance for some one-to-one with Luke.'

'Oh—I suppose there is that.' Kate couldn't believe the sudden lift to her spirits. She smiled. 'So, you'll meet us there?'

'Why don't I collect you and the kids and we'll all travel together?'

That might work. Kate toyed with her collar, thinking and then made a pained face. 'You don't have a car safety-seat for Mia.'

'Oh, yes, I do.' He chuckled and reached out to straighten her collar into place. 'I had one fitted just this morning.'

'You did!'

'Yep.'

'Oh,' she said. Then, 'Oh—' again. She leaned against his chest for a moment. 'Then I guess you're right, Dr O'Connor.' She sent him a tremulous smile. 'This *is* serious business between us.'

'Oh, you'd better believe it,' he murmured, his lips tracking down the side of her throat. 'And when we're done at the fair, we'll go to my place as planned. Deal?'

'Deal,' Kate sighed and snuggled closer.

On Saturday, the weather was perfect for the hay festival. Kate pulled on a pair of her softest, sleekest jeans and a pale-blue, long-sleeved shirt. It was so easy to get sunburned and she wasn't taking any chances.

She smiled as she tucked her feet into comfortable, lightweight trainers, knowing she was excited, happy and so it seemed were her children. They were already out on the front verandah with their little backpacks waiting for Aiden to arrive.

Hearing the beep of his car horn, as he slid into the driveway, Kate gathered up her big shoulder bag stuffed with the paraphernalia all mothers of young children seemed to carry. Her own overnight bag and all that it implied had been carefully packed and was sitting on the end of the bed.

She closed her eyes against a surge of desire.

Tonight, she'd be with Aiden.

'Hi,' she called, walking across the verandah and down the steps.

Aiden was settling Luke and Mia into the back seat of the Landrover. 'Morning.' He glanced back over his shoulder, giving a final hitch to Mia's safety harness.

Kate almost forgot to breathe. He looked so right with her children, so…dad-like, making sure they were comfortably and safely seated, keeping a funny patter going so easily, that even had Luke giving a face-cracking grin. 'Now,' Aiden said, giving Mia's knee a playful little tap. 'We'll just get your mum's gear stowed and we'll be off. Boot's open,' he said in an aside to Kate as he closed the car door.

'OK.' Kate followed him to the rear of the four-by-four.

'This doesn't weigh much.' Aiden took her overnight bag and placed it in beside the children's backpacks.

'I don't need much.'

'Did you pack your jammies?'

Kate rolled her eyes. 'Do I know you?'

Aiden hooked his hands low across her hips. 'Oh, you will, baby…' He was looking at her as though he wanted to devour her. 'By this time tomorrow, you'll know me very well.'

Kate was all thumbs as she drew the seat belt around her and clicked it shut. It was only a thirty-minute drive to Lakeview. She hoped she'd would have recovered her poise by then.

'Have you squared it with your mum about not staying the night there?' Aiden's hand crept across and covered hers.

Kate shook her head, turning her hand over and returning the pressure on his fingers. Emotions hot and heavy swamped her. 'It'll be fine,' she murmured.

Their gazes meshed and she felt a faint heat come to her skin. 'Sure?' He raised a dark brow.'

'Yes.'

'Put your hats on, kids,' Kate directed as they piled out of the car. Even though it was still early, the sun had a bite in it already. They'd found a parking spot at the rear of Lakeview's only coffee shop and the glorious aroma of freshly-brewed coffee floated out on the air. Kate looked at Aiden. 'Fancy a coffee before we get started?'

There was a howl of dissent from the children. 'We want to see the hay things.' Mia tugged at her mother's hand.

'And you said I could see the working models first,' Luke chimed in.

'Well, we don't have to rush off and see everything at once,' Kate cajoled, looking at Aiden over their heads for back-up.

'Oh, I'm with the kids,' he said with a grin. 'I think we should hit the festival.'

'Yay!' The children bounced up and down, much taken with that idea.

Looking at Kate, Aiden shrugged. 'Sorry,' he mouthed, stifling his grin. Then, pulling on a black cap that said *Rescue* across the front, he held out his hands, linking Kate on one side and Mia on the other. Always inquisitive, Luke was content to stride ahead.

'This is nice,' Kate said.

Aiden nodded. 'You bet.'

They shared a smile, then suddenly something changed, as if the world tilted a little on its axis. Kate's smile slipped, driven out by the wave of need that engulfed her.

The hay sculptures were arranged in the shape of a horseshoe which was probably relevant, Kate thought, seeing there was a farrier demonstrating the art of shoeing not too far away. 'Aren't they amazing?' She stopped in front of the last one in the row, a depiction of the fairy tale of The Three Little Pigs.

'Oh, look!' Mia exclaimed. 'The wolf's trying to blow down their straw house.'

'Is hay the same as straw?' Luke wanted to know.

'Uh—' Aiden hesitated. 'Well, it's much the same. It all starts out as fodder for the animals.' He looked at Kate for confirmation.

'Couldn't have explained it better myself,' she teased. 'Now,' she began to shepherd the children in the opposite direction. 'Let's go and say hello to Grammy and Granddad, shall we?'

Kate's tummy began churning as they neared the CWA stall. Introducing Aiden to her parents meant so much to her. Even at her mature age, she wanted their approval. Her mother was at the counter with several other women attending to their customers. 'Oh, good, she's seen us,' Kate said too heartily as her mother stepped from behind the counter and came to meet them.

'Darlings!' Gillian held out her arms to the children who ran to her to be caught in a huge hug. 'Hello, Kate.' Gillian lifted her head and smiled, her gaze a little curious on Aiden in the background.

'Aiden.' Kate swallowed and cleared her throat. 'This is my mother, Gillian North. Mum, this is Aiden O'Connor. He works at the surgery with me.'

'Aiden.' Gillian held out her hand. 'How very nice to meet you.'

'Mrs North.' Aiden's handshake was firm. 'It's good to meet you too.'

'Oh, please, call me Gillian. And here's Dad.'

Gillian waved a hand at her husband and beckoned him into the circle.

'Rob, come and meet Kate's friend, Aiden,' she smiled.

The two men shook hands, a slight look of wariness passing between them.

'We came in Aiden's Land Rover,' Luke said importantly.

'Well, well.' Rob North placed his hands on the little boy's shoulders protectively. 'How was that, young fella?'

'It was good.'

'An' Aiden got a new car seat just for me,' Mia chirped not to be outdone.

'Excellent.' Rob's brown gaze settled gently on his daughter. 'How are you, love?'

'Well, thanks, Dad,' Kate said, giving her father a quick kiss. 'Um—just excuse me a sec. I need a word with Mum.'

A little on edge, Aiden watched covertly as Kate drew her mother aside. There was a murmur of conversation and Gillian suddenly smiled and patted her daughter on the upper arm. Whew.

Aiden let his breath go in a whoosh. The matter of where Kate and the children were staying that night looked sorted.

'Granddad, are you coming to see the working models with me?' Restively, Luke tugged on his grandfather's hand.

Rob North pushed his Akubra back on his head. 'I've a couple of jobs to do for your Grammy first, mate. Can you wait a bit?'

'I'll take him, if you like, Mr North,' Aiden offered.

'Would you mind?'

'I'd be glad to.' He looked down at the small boy. 'Is that OK with you, Luke?'

'It's fine,' Luke said with the resignation of a child twice his age.

'I'll take Mia along to the fashion parade.' Kate had rejoined the circle. She glanced at her watch and then at Aiden. 'Meet you back here in what—an hour?'

'That should give us plenty of time,' Aiden agreed. 'Come on Luke.' He touched his hand to the boy's shoulder. 'Let's find these models.'

Luke was entranced as they moved around the display. Finally he hunkered down and watched the model train go round its track, through tunnels and over bridges until it stopped at the station and then began its journey all over again.

'We went on a train once in the States,' he said.

'Did you?' Aiden parked himself on a hay bale beside the child. 'Was it a long trip or a short one?'

Luke thought for a moment. 'It was a long one, I think. We went on vacation.'

'Do you miss living in the States?' Aiden asked carefully. He didn't want Luke to feel he was being put through a questionnaire but by the same token, he needed to find out what made the kid tick.

Luke lifted his small shoulders in a shrug. 'Some. I have a Grammy and a Grandpa there. And an Uncle Brad and an Aunt Cindy.' He made it sound like *Ant*.

'That's quite a family,' Aiden said. 'And school's going OK here?'

'Yup. I like the sport.'

Aiden's face softened into reflective lines. It was heartening to hear Luke open up. But should he push a little further? He decided it was worth a try—gently of course.

'Your dad was good at sport, wasn't he?'

'Uh-huh. He climbed mountains.'

'I climb mountains too.' Aiden leaned forward, resting his forearms on his thighs.

'You do?' Luke's head whipped round in question.

'I've climbed all over the world,' Aiden said modestly.

'My dad only climbed in the States, I think. He taught Mum to climb.'

'Yes, she told me.'

Luke picked up a small pebble and tossed it away. 'Dad was a good climber. I think Mum was too. She hasn't climbed for a long time now.'

'But your mum was brave enough to try something new and that was a good thing.'

Luke turned his head and looked at Aiden thoughtfully. 'I guess…'

'Come on.' Aiden stood to his feet. 'Let's find

the girls, shall we? I can smell burgers cooking somewhere. Hungry?'

Luke nodded and the two set off.

'What about an early lunch?' Aiden asked when they caught up with Kate and Mia.

'Oh, yes, please.' Kate smile was rueful and she held a hand to her tummy. She turned to the children. 'What about a burger, kids?'

Mia's little mouth turned down comically. 'Could I have a hot dog, please?'

'And me,' Luke echoed.

'Please,' came automatically from their mother.

Aiden chuckled. 'Nothing changes, does it?'

'With kids?' Kate rolled her eyes. 'Probably not. Would you like something to drink? I've water but I noticed one of the local wineries has a stall.'

'Better not.' He regarded her with a combination of regret and wryness. 'But later?'

She nodded but looked away hastily.

The hamburgers were delicious, best beef smothered with onions. 'Fantastic,' Aiden commented, catching a dribble of barbecue sauce as it oozed out of the bread roll. 'I could go another.'

'Do it, then.' Kate smiled indulgently. 'One's my limit. 'But I'd love a cup of tea if you can find any on your travels.'

Aiden got to his feet. 'Kids, want any more to eat—ice-creams maybe?'

'Perhaps later,' Kate said before the children could reply. 'I have some fruit here for them if they're still hungry.'

'Of course you have,' Aiden said, with a chuckle in his voice. He put out a hand and touched her hair briefly before moving away.

Kate had barely begun to enjoy her cup of tea when the public address boomed into life. If there was a doctor present, would he or she please report immediately to the Red Cross tent.

Kate and Aiden stood as one. 'Do you know where the tent is?' Aiden's voice rang with urgency.

'Next door to Mum's stall.' Kate bent over,

gathering her things and shepherding the children quickly.

'I'll get my bag. Could you find out what's going on, Kate? I'll be back as soon as I can.'

'Yes. Go!'

'Mummy…' Mia's little voice broke on a sob.

'It's all right, honey,' Kate soothed. 'You and Luke can stay with Grammy while Mummy goes to see if someone's ill.'

In seconds Kate was pushing her way through the tent flap. 'You called for a doctor.' She addressed the middle-aged woman in the Red Cross uniform. 'I'm Kate Preston.'

'Oh, Dr Preston. Thank goodness!' The woman's face cleared. 'I'm Beris Mills. The patient is a child, a little girl, Maddie Keegan. She's over here with her mother. Beris directed Kate to a bed on the far side of the tent where a child lay, her mother cradling her head.

'What happened Mrs Keegan?' Kate bent to the child. Maddie was obviously in distress, her breathing laboured. Was it an asthma attack?

Kate frowned. No, this was something else entirely.

'She was stung by something. I think it was a bee. She screamed when it happened and then a couple of minutes later, she went all wobbly and then, and then...her breathing went all raspy.' The mother swallowed and bit her lips together. 'What can have happened...?'

'It seems Maddie may have had an allergic reaction to the bee's venom,' Kate said calmly. And if they didn't act fast, the child would be in anaphylactic shock. 'Where did the bee sting Maddie? Did you see?'

'On her upper arm, here.' The mother pointed to the red, rapidly-swelling weal.

Kate saw. Maddie was wearing a cotton singlet. Its brevity had given the bee easy access. Poor little kid. 'Could we have some light over here, please?'

Beris came running with a torch.

'Just direct it on to the wound, please, Beris,' Kate said. 'Good.' And there is was, the minute black dot at the sting site. She needed to remove it fast. While it remained, embedded in Maddie's skin, the entire bee's venom contained in the attaching sack was being pumped into the child's system.

Kate knew what to do. She'd treated dozens of bee stings during her time in the States. But they couldn't afford to hang about. Maddie's breathing was becoming more laboured. In a split-second, Kate had processed her options. She needed a hard object to remove the stinger. Turning aside, she reached into her big handbag and drew out her wallet. Opening it, she took out a credit card.

'What on earth are you doing!' the agonised mother gasped, as Kate began swiping the card gently over the bite area.

'I'm releasing the venom sack from Maddie's skin.' Kate's actions were controlled and presently, the tiny, life-threatening object was visible on the edge of her credit card. 'There it is.' She held it up.

'Oh, God—' The mother burst into tears. 'Will Maddie be all right now?'

She would. As long as Aiden was equipped with an injectable form of adrenaline. Kate considered the options if he wasn't. There weren't many and none she wanted to consider unless things became dire. But surely he'd carry adrenaline if he was the designated MO for the skydiving team. Surely…

She took Maddie's pulse. The result was worrying. The child's throat was beginning to swell.

Hurry, Aiden.

Please, hurry.

'What do we have?' Suddenly, he was there at her elbow, his medical case clutched at his side.

'Anaphylactic shock. Bee sting.'

Aiden took in the child's distress in a second. 'Did you get the stinger out?'

'Yes. But we need to act fast, Aiden.'

You're not thinking of a trache?'

'Only as a last resort. Do you have epinephrine with you?'

Aiden looked questioning for a second and then nodded. 'It's called epipen here.'

Oh, thank heavens. Kate felt herself go limp.

Unprofessional? Perhaps. But treating children always pushed her maternal buttons.

Aiden released the locks on his case and drew out the prepared dose of adrenaline. 'Will you swab, please, Kate?' In a second, he'd administered the life-giving injection. 'There you are, sweetheart,' he said softly. 'This should make you feel much, much better.'

'Could we get an ice-pack on Maddie's arm, please, Beris?' Kate turned to the hovering Red cross worker.

Beris sped away.

It seemed only seconds until Maddie began to stir. Her eyes fluttered open.

For Kate, it was the best sight in the world. 'You're OK, honey,' she soothed. 'Just stay quietly. Your mum's here.'

Mrs Keegan rained kisses over her small daughter's forehead and then looked up, her gaze linking the two doctors. 'How can I ever thank you?' she whispered.

Kate smiled. 'No thanks needed. It was just fortunate Dr O'Connor and I were here today.'

'Yes… What should I do about Maddie now? Will there be, you know—after effects?'

'Let's have a chat about that.' Aiden had found a couple of director's chairs and set them down near the bed. He pressed Kate into one and then lowered himself into the other. 'Maddie may experience some pain for the next few hours but the cold pack will help reduce the swelling.'

'And when she's feeling up to it,' Kate came in, 'it would be helpful if you could clean the area with soap and water. As well, we'll leave you some cortisone cream to apply to the site.'

'Do you live locally, Mrs Keegan?' Aiden asked.

'No.' The mother shook her head. 'We're just visiting from Brisbane. And please call me Leesa.' She looked down at her daughter. 'Should I take Maddie to our own doctor when we get back?'

'You should,' Aiden advised. 'In view of what's happened, Maddie needs a full assessment. Quite likely she'll need to have a course of allergy injections that will desensitise her body to the venom. In all probability she'll have to carry adrenaline with her in case she's stung at any future time.'

Leesa Keegan swallowed. 'It all sounds quite serious. Will…will they show us how to use this injection? I mean Maddie's only nine.'

'They will.' Kate placed a comforting hand on the child's little wrist. 'It'll be very manageable for Maddie and perhaps, she may never have to use it. But better to be prepared, isn't it?'

'Oh, yes,' Leesa said feelingly.

Aiden bent to his his case again. 'I'll give you a note for your doctor, Leesa, outlining the treatment Maddie received today.'

Kate stood to leave. She touched Aiden on the shoulder. 'I'll just collect the kids,' she murmured. 'Meet you outside.'

CHAPTER NINE

'EVERYTHING all right?' Gillian North asked, as Kate arrived back at the CWA stall.

Kate explained what had happened, adding, 'Surely there should have been an ambulance presence here at such a big event?'

'Well there was but they had to attend a road accident nearby. What a blessing you and Aiden were here.'

Kate nodded. 'Aiden's just finishing up. Where are the kids?'

'Dad's taken them off somewhere.' Gillian bustled around. 'Let's get you a cup of tea.'

As they sat over tea and slices of cream sponge, Aiden said, 'Nice work with the stinger. They can be tricky. How did you remove it—finger nail?'

Kate licked the dab of cream off her bottom lip. 'Credit card.'

'Come again?' His eye brow peaked.

'Trick I learned from a paramedic. The card's hard edge is just the thing to ease out the stinger.'

Aiden looked impressed. 'And you thought I might be bored today. Damn,' he muttered when his mobile phone rang. He listened for a moment and then got to his feet, moving away slightly.

Watching Aiden's body language and listening to the questions he was firing into the phone, Kate's brow pleated in a quick frown. The call was obviously work-related and that could mean anything. She felt a swirl of unease, getting to her feet as he ended the call and rejoined her.

'What is it?'

'I'm so sorry, Kate.' Aiden looked torn. 'I have to go. That was a call from the State Emergency Service. There's been an accident on Collier's Bluff. It's a couple of young hikers. They've gone too far near the edge and fallen over.'

'Both of them?' Kate's hand went to her heart.

'They were holding hands. By all the good luck in the world, they've landed on a ledge. But the female is hurt, possibly leg fracture.'

Kate's mind went blank for a second and then she rallied. 'And her companion?'

'Going nuts of course. But his mobile's reception was a bit iffy. Doug at the SES can't get a team there for a while so I said I'd go ahead.'

Kate edged closer to him. 'Why is it up to *you* to go?'

Aiden heard the tremor in her voice. He put out a hand and captured her wrist. 'Because I'm a member of the SES, Kate, and a doctor. I volunteered to attend when I'm needed. This is one of those times. The mountain is not far from here. It's a relatively easy climb. I'll do what I can medically and wait for the SES guys and the ambulance.'

'Then, I'm coming with you.'

Aiden hadn't expected this. He felt a slow crawl of unease in his stomach. 'Kate, I can manage.'

'You have no real idea of the injuries,' she pointed out. 'And you know it's foolhardy to climb on your own! Now, just let me tell Mum what's happening. We don't know how long any of this is going to take, so I'll ask her to keep the kids tonight. Could you get their stuff from the car? Then, we'll set off.'

'Kate, no!' Aiden's mouth tightened. 'Look,' he placated, 'I'll call Brady and see if he can come with me. He's well qualified in mountain rescue.'

'With Jo about to deliver their baby?' Kate shook her head dismissively. 'You can't call Brady out, Aiden. I can pull my weight here. Please, let me.'

For a moment, they stared at each other and Aiden swore under his breath. 'All right,' he growled. 'But if for one moment, I think you're placing your safety in jeopardy, we abort. Agreed?'

Kate looked skywards briefly. 'We're wasting time.'

Aiden drove as fast as the rough bush track would allow.

The nerves in Kate's stomach rose and fell,

steadied. 'I gather it's quicker for us to climb to the accident site than it is to abseil down?'

'By taking this route, it's much quicker.' He sent her a swift, narrowed look. 'Second thoughts?'

'No. Just settling the logistics in my head. You do have gear to fit me out, I take it?'

'I have gear.' Aiden's jaw was clamped. Already, adrenaline was pumping out of him. He feared for Kate. Yet he knew deep down she would not have volunteered to accompany him if she had doubts about her ability. He had to believe that and to go on believing.

'Do you have precise directions where we're to start the climb?' Kate asked evenly. They'd turned in a new direction and already the landscape was changing, thickening to more scrub, more hillocks.

'Doug was able to pin-point it fairly accurately. It's not far now.'

In no time at all, they were at the end of the bush track and Kate was able to see the mountain face where they would attempt the rescue.

She felt relief and a kind of weird familiarity all rolled into one. One look told her Collier's Bluff wasn't the steepest she'd climbed but neither would it be easy. No climb ever was.

'Right, this is as far as we can go. The rest is on foot.' Aiden's expression was set and focused. He turned to Kate and their eyes met. The connection was like tugging on a cord, releasing emotion, raw and as deep as the ocean. Aiden's throat constricted as he swallowed. Is this where I tell her, I love her? Of course not, you idiot. She needed strength here, not distraction. He released his seat-belt with a jerk. 'OK, let's do it.'

With quick precise movements, Aiden began to unload the equipment they'd need. He handed Kate a padded orange safety vest. 'Put this on. It'll help the rescue team identify our position.' He looked down at her feet. 'What about your shoes?'

Oh, heck, she'd forgotten about that. Kate flexed her trainers. The soles were too thick. There was no way she would be able to *feel* the rock's surface and place her feet safely on footholes. She sent Aiden a rueful look. 'They're not going to work, are they?'

'Nope.' He dug into his kit and pulled out several pairs of climbing shoes. 'If none of these fit, you're not coming. Understood?'

Kate understood. But dammit, she make them fit! She took a pair that had a slight downturn to the toe, almost like a ballet shoe. Quickly, she discarded her trainers and pulled on the slipper-like climber's shoe. She stomped around briefly. 'They'll do fine,' she said.

'Sure?'

She nodded.

'No dead space in the heel?'

'They're snug,' Kate said. 'Thanks.'

He grunted an acknowledgment. 'We still have a way to walk so tuck your shoes in the pockets of your vest and put your trainers back on.' He pulled out two sets of harnesses. 'Now let's organise our ticket to ride, shall we?'

Kate stepped into the leg loops and adjusted the swami belt just below her waist. Even though they were facing a medical emergency, a strange excitement was starting to build inside her.

She fingered the belay loop at the front of her belt, so strong it would hold a man's weight with ease. She ran through the logistics in her head. Aiden was going to lead and from the base of the mountain, Kate was belaying him. Her job was to take the rope through a device that would lock the rope off if Aiden fell. Literally, he was placing his life in her hands. The thought sent a new kind of awareness shivering up her backbone.

He trusted her implicitly.

Automatically, they both reached for lightweight helmets. 'You'll need gloves while you're belaying me,' Aiden said. 'These should do the job.' He handed her a pair of leather gloves. Then took a pair for himself for when he would have to belay Kate as the second climber.

Although he'd checked the contents of his trauma kit only recently, Aiden checked it again and seeming satisfied, hitched it up across his shoulders. 'That's it,' he said and hauled out his bag of ropes for the climb.

They still had a fair distance to walk to their starting-off point. 'Watch your step,' Aiden cautioned. 'The ground's uneven and there are a couple of small streams.'

That fact didn't seem to slow him down though, Kate realised. But she kept pace with him all the way to the rocky ridge at the base of the mountain.

'Right, this'll do us.' Aiden assembled his ropes and they each secured themselves with a figure-of-eight knot. Aiden checked her harness and the locking device for the rope once, twice, three times. 'OK, let's see if we can spot our quarry.'

Standing together, staring at the hunch of rock that was facing them, it was as if they were cocooned in isolation, cut off from the rest of the world. Their eyes were trained on the mountain. Searching.

'There they are.' Aiden's voice was quietly calm and he pointed and Kate too could see the little human huddle that was the trapped hikers.

They'd erected a flag of sorts, a strip of colour, a scarf perhaps?

'It's about a hundred feet up,' Kate said.

'Yes.'

All emotional contact was contained in a second. They were now professionals. Doctors on a mission of mercy.

'I wonder if they've seen us,' Kate said.

'I doubt it but just in case…' Aiden snapped a torch out of his backpack and held it aloft, flashing it left, right and back again. 'Maybe the sun will pick up a glint and they'll get the message. The climb itself won't be too difficult. We'll start left and then arc back. That should bring us close to the ledge.' He turned to Kate, the intensity of his blue gaze telling her he'd dropped his guard momentarily until he snapped it back. 'If you need to rest during the climb, do it. Keep it simple and keep it safe. See you up there,' he added quietly, before he edged closer to the base of the mountain to look for his first foothold.

Ever vigilant, Kate watched as he climbed. He was making very good progress. His core balance was perfect, his body supple. He was making it look easy but she knew it wasn't.

Only a fool would think that. Finally, he was where he needed to be and signalled Kate.

Now it was her turn.

She tried without success to do the first move. OK, don't panic. It was an age since she'd done this, she was allowed some time to get set. Lifting her head, she saw a crease, tiny, but useful. She wrapped two fingers over it and pulled herself up. She was away.

She made the next couple of moves successfully and then got stuck again. The leg she had in contact with the rock began to shake. With a groan of frustration, she realised she was placing too much pressure on her calf muscles. So, rest. Think.

She had to get the pressure off but that was difficult when you had nothing but a toehold on Mother earth. She didn't want to fall but even if she did, she wouldn't fall far. Aiden would be there belaying her from above. But falling wasn't in her scheme of things at all.

She tried to recall everything she'd been taught.Obviously, a new strategy was called for here. She turned slightly, leaning her hip into the rock-face. She needed to find a solid grip for her hand. Reaching up with her inside arm, she found a pocket in the rock. Excellent. Now all she needed was a small miracle; what climbers referred to as a *sweet spot* that might be hidden at the back of the pocket, one that would allow her to get depth and a decent hold. She began probing with her fingers, searching for just such a spot. And found it.

She was away again, slowly, methodically.

Watching her progress, Aiden began to breathe more freely. She was good. Gutsy. But the next move would test her. He was close enough to call out directions if necessary. He'd wait. But the wait was proving interminable.

'Come on Kate…' he hissed beneath his breath. 'Put the inside edge of your shoe on a high foot-hold and rock on to it. Attagirl!' She'd done it, shifting her centre of gravity directly over her foot, her move, efficient, clean, beautiful.

Kate stilled, perspiration lodging wetly in the small of her back. One more move and she'd be there. The strength of Aiden's presence seem to call her on. She pressed down on a section of rock, using her shoulder and tricep muscles to push her body up and over to the ledge where Aiden was waiting for her.

'Well done.' His praise was deliberately understated when in reality he was stunned beyond belief with her ability. He pressed his hand over hers. 'Relax and get your bearings, OK?'

For answer, Kate turned her hand over and returned the pressure on his fingers. Emotion and a sense of relief were clogging her throat. She took a moment to gather herself, looking down at the massive wall of rock, the patches of scrubby trees, tracking the path she'd climbed.

And in a light-bulb moment, she knew why she'd made this climb today. It had been sheer instinct, in some way a final salute to Cory. For a second a sense of grief ambushed her but it was overlain with triumph and a sense of rightness.

Here in this amazing explosion of wilderness,

of nature at its fiercest and most beautiful, she could finally let him go.

'Feeling OK?' Aiden asked.

Kate felt her heart lurch. To regain her composure, she breathed in, filling her lungs with crisp mountain air. 'Yes.'

'I figure we've a bit to go yet,' Aiden said. 'The ledge is narrow and there's an angle just there.' He pointed out the craggy over-hang. We'll go on all-fours. That'll be the safest.'

Kate nodded. Her legs felt as loose as a puppet's and there was a crick in her neck that would need a year's worth of massage to shift. But they had a job to do.

Aiden raised his face to the sky, gauging how much daylight they had left. They still had plenty and there was no sign of a storm brewing. 'Good to go, then?' He wrapped his arm around her shoulders and squeezed.

Kate soon realised the going was difficult, the ledge, besides being narrow was littered with shards of rock. Aiden brushed them aside and they crept slowly forward.

'We'll have to inch along on our bellies through here, he said as the overhang of rock loomed closer.

Kate followed his lead, hearing the dull clunk of metal from their harnesses as they crept forward. Even crawling, the space was tight, almost claustrophobic. Kate was beginning to doubt her sanity until she remembered every inch they pushed themselves, was bringing them closer to the trapped hikers. And for them, the waiting to be rescued must be agony, their dread increasing by the minute.

'One more heave should see us through this part, Kate,' Aiden's voice was strained with effort. 'And then we should be where we need to be.'

He was right.

Coming out of the craggy under-hang, Kate dared a look up. The ledge had miraculously widened into a kind of apron and a young man and woman were huddled together not twenty feet away. She and Aiden rose to all-fours again and slowly, painstakingly closed in beside them.

'G'day,' Aiden's mouth quirked at the corner. 'Sorry to be so long getting here. I'm Aiden and this is Kate. We're doctors.'

'Thank God…' The young man's voice broke and then steadied. 'We're Gordon and Amanda.' He shook his head. 'We saw your signal—what a climb you've made. I—we're so grateful—'

'Just doing our job,' Aiden dismissed. 'Listen, mate we need to get some triage going here. How's Amanda doing?'

'I think she's hurt quite badly.' Gordon looked fearfully at his girlfriend. 'It was all incredibly sudden—the fall I mean.'

'It would be.' Kate put a hand sympathetically on the young man's upper arm and it came away bloody. 'You're hurt as well, Gordon?'

'Shoulder. Caught a sharp bit as we fell. Nothing to worry about. Please, just look at Mandy.'

Aiden was already doing that, flicking a penlight into the injured girl's eyes, relieved to see her pupils were equal and reacting. 'Hi Mandy,' he said gently, beginning a test of her competency. 'Can you tell me where you are?' Amanda's answers were disconnected, strained but she got them out.

'Fractured tib for sure,' Aiden said in an undertone to Kate. The young woman was wearing shorts, the bone's displacement clearly visible.

'Will they cope at Mt Pryde hospital?' Kate asked, wondering whether they'd have to summon the CareFlight chopper to transport the injured girl to Brisbane.

'Easily,' Aiden said. 'They'll call Callum O'Byrne in.'

'He's a surgeon?'

'Multi-skilled.' Aiden pulled his mobile out of his back pocket. 'I'll let them know.'

'Awful pain…' Amanda whimpered. 'My leg…'

'Take it easy, honey,' Kate was quietly calm. 'We'll give you something directly.' She popped an oxygen mask over the injured girl's face. 'Breathe in now, Amanda, nice and steady. That's it. Good work. How's her pulse doing, Aiden?'

'Bit shocky but strong enough,' he responded tersely. 'OK to give morphine.' He prepared the injection while Kate swabbed the site. 'Ready?' At Kate's nod, he shot the painkiller home to the girl's uninjured thigh.

Kate let her breath go. Please heaven, Amanda would experience some relief soon. But they weren't out of the woods yet. She was in shock. They had to try to stabilise her before they handed her over to the ambulance.

Kate delved into the trauma kit. 'I'll get a line in, Aiden.'

'Thanks. Then we'll splint.'

'Hang in there, sweetie.' Kate gently stroked a lock of matted fair hair away away from Amanda's forehead. 'This is just a little pin-prick to hook you up to some fluids. You'll be on your way to hospital soon.'

'Keep brave, babes…' Gordon squeezed Amanda's hand.

'I'll take a look at your shoulder now, Gordon,' Kate said. They'd done as much as they could for Amanda. Now all they could do was wait.

He made a face. 'I'm reasonably OK, I think.' Nevertheless, he shrugged off the short-sleeved shirt he was wearing and exposed his injury.

Kate pursed her lips. Gordon had a deep gash from the point of his shoulder to his mid-upper arm. The site was already swelling and dark blue with bruising and still oozing blood.

'Ah—' Gordon attempted a cracked laugh and followed her gaze. 'Will I need stitches, Doctor?'

'You may need a suture or three,' Kate smiled. 'By the way, is that an English accent I can detect there?'

Gordon nodded. 'Mandy and I are on a gap year before we start uni. We've been working our way round Australia. We came here for the crop picking.' He paused. 'All the pickers had today off so we thought we'd do some hiking. We followed the marked trail but we must have moved off course a bit. Well, more than a bit,' he admitted ruefully.

'Accidents happen,' Kate said from the heart. 'Don't beat up on yourself. Just learn from the experience. But for now, let's just get a pressure bandage on your wound. Have you had a tetanus shot lately?'

'Don't think so.'

'They'll probably give you one at the hospital to make sure.'

'Do you do this job all the time?' Gordon wanted to know.

'Climb mountains?' Kate shook her head. 'Not me but Aiden does it fairly regularly.'

'What do I do?' Aiden joined in. He'd been monitoring Amanda and seemed satisfied she was stablising well.

'Search and rescue.' Kate secured the pressure bandage neatly.

'Why do you do it?' The young man's look was clearly admiring.

Aiden shrugged. 'Show-off probably,' he offloaded with a crooked grin. 'Have you left a car here somewhere?'

'At the base.' Gordon looked worried. 'It's a Holden ute, dark blue. What should I do about it?'

'Well, the ambulance will take you and

Amanda straight through to Mt Pryde hospital. So if you're agreeable, I'll inform the local police. They'll arrange to have your vehicle towed to the station. It'll be secure there until you can collect it. Where are you living?'

'We've digs in Mt Pryde and working for Luscombe farms.'

'Then you'd better let your employers know the situation. Neither you nor Amanda will be fit for work for a while. Amanda probably not at all for the rest of the season. Ask the treating doctor at the hospital for a note to that effect.'

The young man nodded, looking suddenly overcome by the enormity of the situation. He leaned his head back against the rock face. 'Mandy's parents will think I'm rubbish after this. They didn't want her to come. But I promised to take care of her…'

Kate felt desperately sorry for him. He was young and bearing responsibility for the girl beside him. And he was on the other side of the world, thousands of miles from home. 'It was an accident, Gordon,' she restated gently. 'And you've done all the right things. You brought your mobile and carried water and you've stayed calm and done as much as you could for Amanda until help arrived.'

'I suppose…' Gordon was pale and tight-lipped. 'But what if you hadn't come?'

'If it hadn't been Kate and me, it would have been someone else,' Aiden said. 'Your call for help would have been answered. Chill out, mate.' He tapped Gordon across his uninjured shoulder. 'It could have been a whole lot worse. Ah, that's our call.' Aiden rocked back on his heels as his mobile rang. 'Right.' He closed off the phone. 'Ambulance and SES are up top. They're sending down a stretcher for Amanda. And Gordon, you'll be winched up in a safety harness.' He turned aside to Kate. 'We'll follow and the SES crew will take us back to our vehicle. Sound OK?'

Kate tipped her face up to the sky, relief and a sense of release flooding through her. 'Very OK.'

'I hope they'll be all right, Aiden,' Kate said.

They were back in his Land Rover and on their way home from the retrieval.

'Of course they will.'

'I'd like to keep tabs on them all the same.'

'Feel free to do it then. But they'll be well looked after by the ED. Callum and Fliss will see to that.'

'What if their families are not supportive?' Kate worried. 'They're so young.'

'Kate, come on! Why wouldn't they be supportive? They seemed nice kids. I'd lay a bet, one or both sets of parents will be over on the first available flight.'

Kate brightened. 'Oh, I hope so.'

'Hey…' Aiden said gruffly, reaching out to lift her hand and press her knuckles to his lips. 'We're off duty now. Could we concentrate on us?'

Kate took a shallow breath, a river of awareness flooding down her spine. She bit down on her bottom lip. 'Of course we could. Um—do we have much further to go?'

'About ten Ks.' Aiden frowned a bit. 'You're still all right with this?'

'Coming home with you?' She'd caught the look on his face and had a moment of insecurity. 'As long as you are?'

His jaw tightened. 'I've always been all right with it. But if you're not, I'll turn the car round now.'

Kate's eyes widened. 'You really would, wouldn't you?'

'It has to be right for you.'

'It is,' she responded softly, unbelievably touched by his honesty. 'Besides,' she added cheekily. 'I want to see this house you've been boasting about.'

CHAPTER TEN

KATE'S first glimpse of Aiden's home was of a long, timber dwelling, the glass expanse of doors all shielded with plantation shutters. There was no formal garden as such. Instead, a long stretch of lawn surrounded the house.

Aiden followed Kate's gaze as she took it all in. 'I haven't had time to get into landscaping. But I figure the bush surroundings make their own statement anyway. I've chucked in a few fruit trees around the back though.'

'The house looks so right there,' Kate's voice was hushed. 'So peaceful. Oh, and look,' she smiled as two small wallabies showed themselves briefly, raising their heads as though listening before bounding off into the sanctuary of the bush. 'What kind of timber did you use for the construction?'

'Dad recommended cedar. It weathers well with time. Come on.' Aiden leaned across and pecked her cheek. 'Let's go inside.'

Kate stepped up on to the wide verandah, moving across to the timber railings. She inhaled the sweet bush scents, her eyes lapping up the breathtaking views of the countryside, full of soft shadows now, in the late afternoon. She felt the stress of the day beginning to roll off her. 'It must be so nice living here…'

Aiden's mouth pleated at the corners. 'As long as you like the bush and don't mind the odd scramble of mating possums on the roof.'

Kate gave an off-key little laugh, the husky timbre of his voice coiling around her. She turned back to the view. 'Mind if I stay here for a bit?'

'Stay as long as you like.' He aimed a kiss into her hair. 'I'll take your bag through.'

A short while later, he was back, his arm pressing against Kate's as she stood at the railings. He looked down at her. 'So… Kate Preston. Here we are…'

'Mmm.' Kate turned her face up and met his gaze. She swallowed, her heart tripped. His eyes looked bluer, ablaze, desire barely kept in check.

She felt the shiver of anticipation bead along the surface of her skin as he bent and pressed a lingering kiss to her temple, the side of her throat and finally her lips. 'I've run a bath for you…'

Her throat went dry. 'That's nice…'

'Let's go in, then.'

Kate was enchanted by the feeling of light and space as they moved along the soft timbered flooring and entered what was obviously his bedroom. It was lovely, the furnishings simple and understated like the timber bed with its dark blue quilt and the cane bedside tables. Kate tilted a smile at him. 'I'd no idea there were so many shades of white. It's perfect.'

He looked pleased. 'Works well, doesn't it?' He ushered her through to the ensuite bathroom. 'I think you'll find everything you need.'

Lord. How could she not? The whole place was sumptuous. Her gaze went to the modern-look clawed bath set beside two picture windows that looked out across the blue-green of the valley. 'Wow…' She moved closer. 'I may never want to get out. And bubbles!' She arched her brows. 'For me?'

'I was reared in a family of females.' He lifted a shoulder in a casual shrug that didn't fool Kate for a second. 'I know about girls and their bubble baths.'

'Well, it's a lovely thought.' Kate's nerves were beginning to shred around the edges. She took a deep breath and let her heart do the talking. 'Thank you, Aiden.'

'For what?'

'For making me feel—I don't know—so special, I guess.'

'You *are* special, Kate.' He reached out and cupped her cheek. 'Enjoy your bath. I'll bring you a glass of wine in a bit.'

'Make it a small one.'

He held up a finger in response and left.

Kate shed her clothes and slid into the luxurious warmth of the foamy water. Closing her eyes, she found a comfortable spot on the porcelain and gave herself up to the moment. Usually she wasn't self-conscious about her body but now it mattered. She was here with the man she loved. And they were about to exchange the most intimate gift of all. And he was gorgeous. Sexy. So very male…

'Kate…?'

She opened her eyes to see the man of her dreams there beside her. She blinked a bit. He'd obviously showered, his hair still damp and spiked, his torso bare above the towel wrapped round his waist.

Kate allowed a shallow breath to escape. 'You look like you've just stepped out of the jungle in your lap-lap.'

He parked himself on the edge of the bath. 'I figured a suit might have been a bit formal. Here's your drink.' He held the fluted wine glass out to her.

'Lovely.' She put out her hand to receive it, revealing the naked curve of her breast as it peeped out of the bubbles. She saw Aiden's gaze rivet and intensify.

They exchanged a long, probing glance, until he said, 'I hardly dare believe you're here with me, Kate.'

'Oh, I'm here.' She took a mouthful of her wine and looked at him over her glass. 'If you want to hang about, I'll prove it to you later,' she teased, suddenly feeling the power of her womanhood.

His eyes flared. 'I'm counting on it.'

'Is this a local wine?' she asked and took another mouthful. 'It's very nice.'

His mouth quirked a bit. 'Are you intending to stay in there all night?'

'Just until I finish my wine.'

'Just drink up, then,' he growled.

She did and then held the glass out to him. 'Would you pass me a towel, please, Aiden?'

He swung round, placing the glass on the nearby vanity and stood to his feet. 'Take my hand.'

Kate blinked uncertainly. She looked at his outstretched hand and shook her head.

'Don't hide from me, Kate.' His plea was soft, urgent.

Kate opened her mouth to say something, then closed it. Her nerve ends were zinging. But he was right. They'd come too far for her to start feeling modest. Nevertheless, she still felt a pang of vulnerability as she took his hand and rose from the foam like a proud Aphrodite.

'Oh, Kate… You're so beautiful,' he murmured hoarsely.

She held her head high, stepping close to him, deliberately putting her hands to his waist and removing his towel. 'And you,' she murmured, her gaze lapping up the sleek perfection of his maleness. 'So beautiful.' She went to him then, arching her body against him and then leaning back, stroking across the firm muscled power of his chest and dark flat nipples until they pebbled under her fingertips. She felt a new sense of empowerment, free, her senses charged, her pulse skipping beats. 'Towel me dry,' she said huskily, her breath coming faster.

He made a sound like a groan. 'This first…'

'Aah…' Kate gave a shallow gasp, feeling her breasts grow heated and swollen and a squeezing sensation at her innermost core as he lowered his head. She made a tiny inarticulate sound in her throat, grasping him more tightly and then feeling her muscles go limp. She hung there, her senses spinning.

Aiden raised his head, his eyes heated and dark. 'You've undone me completely, Kate—is it the same for you?'

'Better,' she affirmed breathlessly. 'I need you, Aiden. Now. Please…'

In a few steps they were on his bed, locked together, skin on skin.

Kate was lost, drifting, a new dimension claiming her as Aiden caressed all her secret places until she was dazed with emotion, ready for him. And when he plunged deep inside her, she cried out, holding on by a thread, climbing ever higher, until they were fragmenting and he was there with her, tumbling into a blinding oneness.

For a long time afterwards, they lay entwined. Replete.

Finally, Aiden stirred. Propping himself up on one elbow, he looked down at Kate, his heart in his eyes. 'We belong together. You know that, don't you?'

She reached out, tracing over his cheek and outlining his mouth. 'I know that now.' Sudden tears hovered at the corners of her eyes and then spilled on to her cheeks.

'Oh, Katie...don't.' Aiden gathered her close again. After a minute he asked, 'Want to talk about it?'

She swallowed, the ache in her throat making it difficult to speak. 'It's been a long time for me. I've wondered if it would ever happen again—to be so in love with someone...'

He gazed steadily at her. 'And it has?'

'Oh, yes.' She put up her hands and swept her tear-drenched lashes. 'I love you, Aiden.'

He touched her hair, smoothing it back from her temple. 'I've waited so long to hear you say that. I think I fell a little in love with you from the start. And it kept getting stronger until I didn't know whether I was on my head or my backside.'

'That must have felt awkward.'

'I felt punch-drunk half the time wondering, hoping you'd love me back. God—' He threw himself back on the pillow. 'It's a miracle, isn't it?'

'Hyperbole, more like.' Kate laughed low in her throat. 'But it's lovely, whatever it is.'

'And *you're* lovely, Kate Preston.' He drew her close again so she could feel the heat off his skin. He sent her a rakish grin. 'Think we could do it again?'

'Oh, I think we could.' Her lips feathered kisses all over his face and down the tanned column of his throat. 'But slowly. I think this time we should go very slowly.'

'Is this where I ask if I can borrow one of your shirts?' Kate joked. It was much later and they'd showered and returned to his bedroom.

'Help yourself.' With a flourish he slid back the door of the walk-in robe.

'Oh, my God…' Kate's eyes went wide in laughing disbelief. 'How many shirts do you have, O'Connor?'

'A few.' He grinned and lifted a shoulder in careless understatement. 'I like my shirts. You'd look good in that one.'

'Mmm.' Kate considered the dark red shirt he'd pulled out. 'No offence, doctor but I think I prefer my sarong.' So saying, she went across to her overnight bag he'd left on the window seat.

'Ah—much more you,' Aiden approved, watching as she took out a swirl of pink and purple silk and draped it prettily over her curves. 'Come on.' He held out his hand to her. 'Let's rustle up some food. You must be starved. I know I am.'

'Well, one way and another we used up a lot of calories today,' Kate said.

'You mean climbing the mountain?' he dead-panned.

She sent him an arch look. 'What else?'

'Kitchen.' He announced proudly and guided her in.

'Oh, my…' Kate looked around the expanse of sleek white fittings and the dusky red tiles on the splash-back.

His eyebrow shot up. 'You like?'

'It's lovely.' She touched her hand to the bench top. 'You didn't go for the stainless steel look, then?'

'God, no!' He pretended to shudder. 'Reminds me too much of the OR. Give me homely every time. Work for you?'

'Definitely.' She cupped her hand on his cheek. 'Now, what do you have to eat?'

Kate put together some nibbles while Aiden set about cooking her the *best steak* she'd ever tasted.

'More of that wine in the fridge,' he said, stopping to smudge a kiss on her bare shoulder on his way to the grill.

'Lovely, thanks.' Kate sent him a quick smile. 'Beer for you, I imagine?'

'Ah—yes, please. And then I'll put on some music. What do you like to listen to?'

'I don't think I'll tell you.' Kate scooped some brie on to a cracker and popped it in her mouth.

'Surely you're not a closet heavy metal fan?'

Kate tsked. 'Is that likely?'

Aiden peppered his steaks and chuckled. He set the timer and then joined her at the breakfast bar, sliding on to one of the high stools. 'Thanks for this.' He took a piece of cheese and a handful of grapes from the platter she'd set out. 'Now, music.'

Kate tilted her head regarding him speculatively. 'You mightn't have what I like.'

'Believe me, I'll have it.' He took a mouthful of his beer.

'Cory introduced me to classic country. That's what I like.'

'Uh-huh.' Aiden's expression didn't alter. 'So Cory was a country boy, then?'

'Through and through.' Kate smiled, her gaze soft. 'He played guitar. Sometimes, we'd sit out on the porch in the moonlight and he'd play.'

'I have some Neil Young,' Aiden said evenly. 'Will that do?'

'Perfectly.' Her smile beamed higher and then it stopped as suddenly as a scudding rain shower. 'Oh, Aiden…' She looked appalled. 'I shouldn't have said all that about Cory. It just slipped out—I'm sorry.'

'Kate.' Aiden put his hands on her shoulders and turned her to face him. 'Don't ever think you can't talk about Cory to me. He was a large part of your life. You had children with him. You wouldn't be human if you didn't think about him sometimes. I understand that.'

'But my timing was awful! We've just made love and you've been amazing. I wouldn't want you to think I was making comparisons or—'

Aiden stopped her quite simply by kissing her. Then he lifted his head and looked into her eyes. 'That thought doesn't deserve head room. I'm not threatened by your past, Kate.' He lifted a hand and knuckled her cheek. 'Cory was good to you, wasn't he?'

Kate nodded. 'Yes, he was good to me.'

'Then, that's all I need to know.' He swung off

the stool, taking her with him. 'Now, this music. Let's find something we can dance to.'

'What about your steaks?'

'We can spare a few minutes.'

'Then, I'll make a salad to go with the steaks.'

'Ah—' His mouth turned down comically. 'I was thinking more in terms of an egg and chips.'

'Aiden…' She took a frustrated little breath, then saw he was laughing at her.

He kissed her on the nose. 'You reel in so beautifully, Kate.'

'And you need someone to monitor your cholesterol,' she shot back. 'But I might—just might microwave you a jacket potato.'

'Then, I'm a lucky man,' he said with a grin.

They made love again during the night, re-enforcing their new-found joy in each other.

Morning came in softly and Kate stirred. Opening her eyes, she blinked. Aiden was sitting on the edge of the bed beside her.

'Morning,' he smiled and kissed her lightly.

Her eyes widened in query. 'You're dressed. Is everything all right?'

'Yes. Come and watch the sunrise with me.'

Barely awake, Kate tried to focus. 'I was planning a sleep-in.'

'You've the rest of your life to sleep in,' he cajoled. 'Come on. The sun won't wait.'

She made a face. 'I need a shower.'

'Two minutes.' He held up the appropriate number of fingers.

Kate swung out of bed. 'So no time for coffee, either?'

'I've made a flask. We'll take it with us.' He propelled her towards the ensuite. 'I'll bring the car round.'

Barely five minutes later, Kate joined him in the Land Rover. She was twisting her hair into a scrunchie.

'You *were* quick.' Aiden seemed impressed.

'Ingrained from my intern years.'

He gave a throaty chuckle. 'I remember those. You got a rocket if you were late on the wards.' He sliced her a quick look. And again. 'You're not ticked off with me for dragging you out of bed, are you?'

'I suppose not.' She gave a rueful half-laugh. 'But I've seen sunrises before, Aiden. This had better be special,' she warned as he took off down the driveway and then launched off on to a bush track.

'It'll be special,' he promised. 'And I've wound the windows down so you can smell the bush. Nothing quite like it.'

Kate began to take an interest in her surroundings. The bush at this early hour seemed full of secrets and a faint mist had come down, resting like a lace shawl on the distant mountains.

She realised they'd detoured into a belt of thick scrub, the air drumming with the sound of cicadas. Then they were in the clear again, spotted gums leaping out of nowhere like sentinels. With quick, deft precision Aiden shot the Land Rover up a steep incline and stopped. 'This'll do us,' he said.

'Oh, yes…' Kate breathed, looking down into the blue-green valley now blistered with pools of light as the first pale rays of sunshine overlapped the bush.

'Magic, isn't it?' Aiden agreed. 'If we sit on the bonnet, we'll get the best view.'

'This is truly awesome,' Kate murmured a few minutes later. The last vestige of dawn had left the valley and all the ochres, the myriad shades of green in the landscape were beginning to come alive, shimmering as a brilliant burst of sun spanned the horizon.

They finished their coffee in silence and then Kate handed Aiden her mug. 'You were right. It was special.'

'We're not finished yet,' he said. 'If we stay very quiet, we may see lyrebirds.'

'Here?' Kate whispered. 'You have lyrebirds here?'

He nodded. 'They don't seem to follow a pattern and I've seen them only rarely. So if they come out this morning, then we're truly blessed.'

Kate's hand slid under his T-shirt finding his warm skin. 'I already feel very blessed, Aiden.'

'Sweet.' Aiden turned his head, his look soft.

Then he tensed slightly and put his finger to his lips. 'Look.'

'Oh…' Kate found she was holding her breath, as two hens appeared out of the bush. They trod warily, pale brown feathers almost lost in the backdrop as they tiptoed across the clearing. 'They're so quaint,' Kate marvelled.

'And here comes the male.'

'Oh, yes…' Kate pressed Aiden's arm, as the male bird stalked after his hens, his bright feathered tail stretched out behind him. 'Will he display?'

'Not this morning, I think. See, there they go.'

'Oh.' Kate was clearly disappointed. The lyrebirds had disappeared as quietly as they'd appeared, blending into the bush in seconds.

Kate inhaled a ragged little breath and tipped her head up to the sky. 'I'll always remember this.'

Aiden shot her a narrowed blue look. 'You sound like it's been a one-off, Kate. We can come again. And again. Bring the kids too.'

Kate felt her stomach lurch. For hours and

hours it seemed, her children had been far from her thoughts. Being with Aiden had totally consumed her. She felt guilty suddenly and took her mobile out of her shirt pocket. 'Talking of kids, I should call Mum.'

'You mightn't get much of a signal here.' Aiden said.

'I'll check for texts anyway. Oh, bless!' She turned to Aiden, her face alight. 'There's one from Jo. She's had her baby, a little girl!'

'Fantastic news. Brades will be over the moon.'

'Born at three o'clock this morning,' Kate passed on.

'And she's already texting?'

Kate gave a Mona Lisa smile. 'She'll be on a high. There's no feeling quite like it. You've delivered your baby and you feel relieved and thrilled and amazingly proud.' She rolled her eyes expressively and laughed. 'It's probably just endorphins kicking in but who's going to tell a new mum that?'

'Well not me,' Aiden said a bit too heartily. Hell. He clamped his jaw, almost feeling a muscle twang. He felt suddenly at a loss. He couldn't identify with what Kate was saying. But then, he reasoned, what male actually could. At the thought, he felt marginally cheered.

They spoke little on the way home. When they went inside Aiden said, 'Why don't you call your mum? I'll rustle up some breakfast.' A little while later, he looked up as Kate came into the kitchen. 'Everything OK?'

Kate eyes slid away. 'Mmm. What can I do to help?'

'I thought we'd eat out on the deck.' Aiden checked the scrambled eggs in the pan. He'd seen the tiny frown in her eyes but he'd chosen to ignore it. If Kate wanted him to know anything, she'd tell him. But the possibility of her being worried niggled at him. It would have to be about her kids of course. He tried to push the intrusion away. Selfishly, he wanted Kate to himself for just a while longer. Surely that wasn't too much to ask?

Yes, it was. Kate and her children came as a package. He'd known that from the start.

Shape up, O'Connor, he self-directed and his jaw clenched again. It was time he got the message. Love Kate. Love her kids.

They finished tidying the kitchen after breakfast.

'You've gone quiet, Kate,' Aiden said, watching her fold the tea towel neatly over its rack. 'Is something worrying you?'

Kate didn't try to prevaricate. 'Mum said Luke has been asking a lot of questions.'

'About?'

'My whereabouts mostly.'

'But surely he knows you're here with me?'

Kate nodded.

'And that's a problem for him?'

Kate hesitated, hearing his query like a giant resonance in the air. 'Possibly.'

Aiden blew out a controlled breath. 'I've tried to walk a middle ground with him. I think he's responding. And he seemed fine with me at the hay festival.'

'But I was there too,' Kate said, as if that explained everything.

A beat of silence.

'OK... With hindsight, I guess we could have doubled back and picked the kids up from your parents' when we'd got down off the mountain yesterday,' Aiden reasoned slowly. 'Then we could have all come back here as originally planned.'

'I thought about that...' Kate's heart beat accelerated. 'I knew you'd have done exactly that if I'd asked you.'

A frown etched sharply between his eyes. He wasn't understanding any of this. 'Then, why didn't you?'

'Because—' She blinked and her throat closed tightly. 'Because deep down I wanted this time alone with you, Aiden. I *needed* it. And when circumstances played into our hands, I ran with the possibility. Do you think that makes me a bad mother?' Her eyes were pleading, a bit desperate.

'Oh, Kate...' Aiden reached out and drew her

close. 'How could you even begin to think that? You're a brilliant mother. But you're a woman too.' He leaned back to look at her. 'Go easy on yourself. You're allowed a life apart from your children.'

'It doesn't work like that, Aiden. I'm the only parent Luke and Mia have now. While they're so young,I have to put their needs before my own.'

'But not to the exclusion of everything and everyone else. I want to make a life with you, Kate.' Aiden tightened his arms around her. 'I thought you understood that.'

Well, she did and she didn't. 'But all this stuff with Luke…' A flicker of uncertainty crossed her face.

He stroked the side of her face. 'We'll sort it out. What would you like to do now, go out to your parents' place and collect the kids? We can bring them here for the day.'

'No.' Kate stepped away, her tone resolute. 'I'd like you to take me home, please, Aiden. I'll go and collect the children, spend the day with them. It'll be better that way.'

'For whom?'

'Aiden, please don't push this.' Kate held her ground. 'We have to do this gradually. Luke and Mia have to get used to you being around and to get to know you.'

'And how are we going to do that if we're not even together?' He looked baffled, even a bit grim.'I think you're making too much of Luke's reaction. He's a child for heaven's sake!'

'He's *my* child,' Kate shot back. 'His feelings matter.'

'Hell, Kate—' Aiden spun away, tunnelling his hands through his hair in frustration. 'I can't believe we're even having this conversation.'

They looked at each other for a long frozen moment until Kate broke the tension. 'I'll just get my things.'

Aiden waited a minute and then followed her into the bedroom. He looked at the ummade bed, the tossed sheets and thought of the wild passion they'd shared. 'Kate…' he felt a lump in his throat the size of a lemon. 'Don't leave like this, with things so unsettled between us.'

Kate's hands fumbled as she pushed the last of her things into her overnight bag and closed the zip. She turned to face him. 'If you're already resenting my son, Aiden, we don't seem to have much of a future, do we?'

'I don't resent him!' Aiden's blue eyes flashed like lasers. 'I think Luke is a great kid. He's bright and savvy, probably a bit too savvy. But Kate, we can't be held to ransom by an eight-year-old child.'

CHAPTER ELEVEN

MONDAY morning.

How were they going to get past this? Aiden wondered grimly as he arrived at the surgery. He was early but so was Kate. He'd seen her car in its parking space.

One small boy equalled one large headache. That was all he knew for certain. 'I'm in this for the long haul,' he'd told Kate yesterday when he'd driven her home. She hadn't seemed reassured. Instead, she'd questioned his actual readiness to have children in his life at all.

And that had hurt.

With his stomach resembling the inner workings of a cement mixer, he walked along the corridor to Kate's consulting room. He knocked and poked his head in. 'Morning.'

Kate squeezed her eyes shut for a second before she looked up from her computer screen. 'Aiden.' She swallowed unevenly. 'I didn't expect you so early.' She beckoned him in. 'Do you want to sit for a minute?'

For answer, Aiden leaned back against the wall and folded his arms. 'Did you make any progress with Luke?'

Lord, she wished he wouldn't do this. Be so confrontational. 'It wasn't the time. We just had our usual Sunday together.'

'Cosy, was it?'

His voice contained a thread of bitterness and Kate's gaze sharpened. Then, quite deliberately, she swung off her chair and went to stand in front of him. 'Aiden, this is not something that's going to be resolved in a day or a week.'

'It's not going to be resolved at all if we don't work at it. *Together.*' Aiden's voice rose in frustration. 'I need to be involved, Kate. Surely, you can see that?'

Kate stayed silent,suddenly too close to the edge to answer. She felt jaded and torn. Terribly torn between her son and her lover. Pain welled in her heart. She'd never wanted to find herself in this position. Never. 'I hardly know what to think any more...' Her composure began to crumple. 'I couldn't sleep...'

'Join the club.' He laughed, a short painful sound. 'It seems all I'm doing is making you unhappy...'

'Oh, you're not!' Kate's eyes flew wide in denial. 'Don't think that for a second. I want this to work, Aiden.'

'Then you have to trust me.'

Kate's mouth trembled. 'It's—just hard to start letting go, handing over some of the responsibility.'

'I get that, Kate.' Aiden pulled a stream of air into his lungs and let it go. 'If I seem to be pushing you, it's because I want some certainty in our relationship.'

'I want that too.' Kate looked at him, her dark eyes pleadingly soft.

'OK...' Aiden placed his hands on her shoulders and squeezed. 'How can we accomplish the outcome we want? I'll do whatever it takes, Kate.'

There was a pause. 'Well,' Kate said finally, 'perhaps if the children get used to seeing us together, doing stuff together, it will begin to normalise things.' At his raised eyebrow, she added hastily, 'I realise they're small steps.'

'But better than none at all. Oh Katie…' He pulled her close. 'I thought I'd made a hash of things.'

'No.' She gave a definitive shake of her head. 'It takes two to make a hash of things. Relationships are tricky at the best of times but with children involved, ours is just a bit trickier. And we should remember that.'

'My wise Kate.' He tenderly tucked a tendril of hair behind her ear. 'So, from now on, we keep the communication lines wide open. Agreed?'

'Agreed.' Kate touched his face, stroking the marks of strain around his eyes with gentle fingertips. 'I hated the way we parted yesterday.'

'It was brutal,' he agreed. 'I went home and chopped enough wood to last a year.'

'Oh, Aiden…' Kate didn't know whether to laugh or cry as she imagined it. 'From now on, we'll do better,' she promised.

'Yes, we will,' he agreed fervently. 'Very much better.'

Two months later on a Sunday afternoon, Kate decided they could congratulate themselves. They *had* done better. They were spending time together both at her house and at Aiden's. The children seemed settled, happy with the arrangement. Luke had joined a football team and seemed to be showing a natural skill, with some extra tuition from Aiden of course…

'Watching our champ?' Aiden joined her on the wooden bench seat on his front veranda.

She turned and smiled at him. 'He's pretty good now,' she said with a mother's pride, watching Luke dribbling his football across the front lawn. 'Thanks to you.'

'It's nothing.' Aiden gave a self-effacing little snort. 'It's been the best time of my life having you and the kids here with me.'

Kate felt cocooned in a little bubble of happiness. She snuggled closer, leaning her head against his shoulder. This place was magical. Her eyes grew wistful as she looked out at the line of blue hills, the green paddocks and the little gullies with their brush of wild plum and silky oak. And she'd seen the wallabies again this morning, so innocently beautiful with their lush brown pelts and little pointed faces. She gusted a sigh. 'I could never tire of this place.'

'Then make your home here,' he invited quietly. 'Marry me.'

Kate sat up, blinking fast. She opened her mouth and closed it.

'Share your life with me, Kate. All of it.' Aiden was looking at her intently, his blue eyes alight with caring, with love. Such love.

Kate found her voice at last. Being with Aiden was wonderful. Right. He was her love. Her heart sang with joy. 'Yes.'

'Yes?'

'Yes.' Kate smiled mistily. 'Yes.'

With a whoop, Aiden whirled them upright. He

gathered her into a fierce bear-hug, feeling tiny tendrils of her hair tickle his nose. They pulled away and grinned at each other.

'Let's tell the kids,' they said in unison.

Two weeks later, Kate was wearing a beautiful ring and they'd booked the church for their wedding in six weeks time. Jo and Brady had been delighted to accept their invitation to be their witnesses, Jo declaring she almost had her figure back and that she and Kate must go shopping for dresses very soon.

Life couldn't get much better, Kate thought as she settled into work that Monday morning. Only an hour later, she was in a state of disbelief. Ascertaining from Vicky that Aiden was between patients, she hurried along to his room.

'Kate?' Startled by her sudden entrance, Aiden swung up from his chair. 'What's happened?'

'It's Luke…' Kate's voice was thin with distress. 'He's in trouble at school.'

'Hey…come here.' Aiden took her upper arms and steadied her. 'Just tell me.'

'He's hit another boy.' Kate took a shaken breath. 'In the mouth. There was blood.'

'Ah.' Aiden digested the information quietly. 'Maybe the kid deserved it.'

Kate looked appalled. 'He can't go round hitting people, Aiden. I don't understand it.' She shook her head. 'It's—so out of character for him—

'Have you been summoned to the school?'

'Not exactly. The head teacher said he'd like a chat after school but I've no patients booked until eleven so I said I'd go across now.' Aiden looked torn. 'I'd come with you but I've a consult due. Couple with fertility issues. I can't reschedule them.'

'No, of course you can't.' She broke away. 'I'll be fine.'

'I'll walk you to your car.'

'No.' She turned back, agitatedly running her fingers down his shirt front. 'Wait for your patients, Aiden. I can handle this on my own.'

But she shouldn't have to. Watching her leave hurriedly, Aiden felt he'd let her down somehow.

Luke again. He'd thought he'd got the lad sorted. But obviously not. It worried him.

It was lunch time before they were able to speak privately.

'So, what happened at the school?' Aiden asked. They gone across to the park and were seated at one of the picnic tables.

Kate looked bleak. 'Luke wouldn't tell me anything. Apparently, at the teacher's insistence, he mumbled an apology to this other boy, Justin, but his teacher said, clearly, he didn't mean it.'

'Kate, kids, boys especially often have a biff in the schoolyard and then it's forgotten.'

'But I don't want some pattern of aggressive behaviour developing, Aiden.'

He leaned across and squeezed her hand. 'I'll talk to Luke man to man. It'll sort itself, Kate.'

But by the end of the week, it hadn't. Luke had steadfastly refused to tell Aiden anything, his stubborn manner almost hostile. Aiden refused to let it get to him. Kate and the kids were spending the weekend with him at Three Oaks. Luke would open up there. Aiden was sure of it.

On Saturday morning, Luke announced to his mother,' I don't want to go to Aiden's place.'

Kate felt her heart hitch. 'He's expecting us, Luke.' She eyed her son carefully. 'You're not sick, are you?'

The boy shook his head.

'Then, get your backpack,' Kate said firmly. 'We're leaving shortly.'

'Don't press him,' Kate said urgently to Aiden after they'd arrived and the children had gone to play outdoors.

Aiden's mouth drew in. 'Still nothing?'

'No. He just seems unhappy. It can't go on, Aiden.'

'Hell, Kate.' Aiden massaged a hand across his forehead as if to clear his thinking processes. 'If you don't want me to press him, then what else can I do?'

'Do you think it has something to do with the wedding?'

Aiden drew back sharply. 'What makes you think that?'

'He's changed since we told told him we were getting married.'

'We're not postponing the wedding.' Aiden's eyes were suddenly flint-like. 'Luke has to realise he doesn't run this family.' He strode out.

Kate shut her eyes and sighed sharply. Already the day seemed ruined. Later, she cobbled some lunch together although she knew neither she nor Aiden would feel like eating. 'Mia, go and call your brother, please?' she said to her daughter who was hovering, fussing with her dolls.

Several minutes later, Mia was back. 'I can't find Luke,' she said to her mother. 'I called and called.'

Kate felt a ripple of unease that quickly turned into an avalanche. She downloaded a sparkly smile at Mia. 'Hey, your favourite TV programme is on about now.'

'Yay.' Mia skipped off happily.

Kate's heart seemed to be jostling for space inside her chest, as she ran across to the small barn that Aiden currently used as a garage for his Land Rover. She stopped at the door, a tiny sound like a whimper escaping her mouth.

Aiden spun round from the bench where he was working. 'Kate?'

'Luke's missing.' Kate bit down on her lips to stop them trembling. 'Did you speak to him?'

'No—I decided to wait. I thought we'd speak with him together. Sweetheart, it'll be all right.' In a few steps Aiden had her in his arms. She sagged against him.

'It mightn't be all right, Aiden. I made him come today. He didn't want to. What have I done…?'

'Calm down, Kate.' Aiden became her rock. Strong. Reliable. He looked deeply into her eyes. 'Luke is making a statement. He wants help. He just doesn't know how to ask for it. I have a fair idea where he may have gone. I'll find him. Remind me again what colour shirt he's wearing.'

Kate took a jagged breath. 'Blue. He—might be hurt, Aiden.'

'And I'm a doctor. Kate, go back to Mia. Please.

'Little monkey,' Aiden growled, as he made a beeline for the gully. They'd had rain during the week. He guessed it had refreshed the creek that ran seasonally. He knew it was one of Luke's favourite places. Well, let's hope he'd chosen it today, he thought grimly.

He reached the top of the incline and looked down. The outline of the gully was clearly visible, lush and green, easy for a kid to hide. He began to make his way down. Soon his steps had carried him to the flat and the bed of the creek.

He kept walking, ducking under the low-hanging bottlebrush and pushing back the whippy branches of the wild plum. He kept his eyes peeled and finally he was rewarded. A flash of blue through the foliage. Luke's T-shirt.

Aiden took a deep, steadying breath and went forward carefully. How he handled things in the next few minutes could change all of their lives. And not in a good way.

But he wouldn't think like that.

Pushing back the last trail of branches, he came within a few yards of his quarry. Keep it low key, Aiden told himself. 'Hey, there, Luke?'

The boy's head jerked round. He looked panicked for a moment and then he turned back. 'Hey,' he said, barely audibly.

'It's lunch time.' Aiden lowered himself on to the creek bank beside the boy. 'Are you hungry?'

Luke shrugged, watching the ebb and flow of the switch he was trailing in the water.

Aiden made himself comfortable, linking his arms across his raised knees. 'Seen any fish?'

'Tiny ones.' Luke kept his face averted.

'Do you like to fish?' Aiden asked.

'Granddad takes me fishing to the dam sometimes.'

'Uh-huh. I like surf fishing. We could try that sometime if you'd like to.'

Luke showed a flicker of interest. 'Where would we go?'

'Down to the coast. School holidays are coming up. We could go then.'

Silence.

'Luke, listen to me,' Aiden said gently. 'You've got a burr in your britches about something, so how about you tell me? No-one is mad at you. But unless we talk about things, we can't fix them. That makes sense, doesn't it?'

'I don't want you and Mum to get married,' Luke blurted out.

Well, surprise, surprise. 'Mind telling me why?'

Luke's small shoulders lifted as he took a huge, agonised breath. ''Cos I'd have to change my name an' I don't want to.'

Aiden was appalled that something so innocuous had rendered the youngster so traumatised. Poor little kid. 'Who told you that?'

'Kid at school.'

'Justin?'

Luke nodded. 'He was in my face all the time. 'Cos his mum got married and he had to change his name an' he said I'd have to. An' when I said I wouldn't, he started calling me, Luke No-name. He wouldn't shut up…'

'So you whacked him.'

Luke nodded.

'Oh, good grief,' Aiden ground out under his breath. 'Come here, matey.' He looped out an arm and drew the boy in. 'Now, for starters, just because your mum and I are getting married, it doesn't mean you have to change your name. You will always be Luke Preston. Always.'

'Are you sure?' Luke's voice was small.

'I'm very sure. You have your Dad's name and that's how it will stay.'

'But you're going to be my dad now, aren't you?' Luke eyed Aiden squarely, his voice wobbling a little.

Oh, boy. He should have consulted a child psychologist before he'd embarked on any of this. Aiden took his time to find the right answer. If indeed, there was one. 'I'd like to be your dad. I think we make a good team, don't you?' He flashed a grin at the earnest little face of Kate's son. 'We do good stuff together. I like having you around.'

That seemed to please Luke. 'Did Mum pick you 'specially?' he wanted to know.

'Ah—' Aiden gave an embarrassed laugh. 'We kind of picked each other I guess.'

'So, will Mum change her name, then?'

'Dunno.' Aiden shrugged. 'We haven't talked about it. I guess she may want to add my name to hers and call herself, Dr Preston-O'Connor.'

Luke actually managed a trapped smile. 'That'd be a long name.'

'Sure would.' Aiden lifted a hand and ruffled the little boy's hair. 'What say we leave it up to Mum, shall we?' After a while, Aiden said, 'Is anything else bothering you?'

A beat of silence until Luke said hesitantly, 'Maybe.'

'Uh-huh.' Aiden controlled his breathing, while his heart bucked with a new unease. And he wondered how Kate managed this parenting gig with such insight. But he fancied himself as a fast learner. He gave Luke's shoulder a little nudge. 'Better talk the talk, then buddy. What is it?'

'You go sky-diving, don't you?'

'Sometimes.' Aiden's senses sharpened. 'Is that a problem for you?'

Luke's brown eyes, so reminiscent of Kate's turned soulfully on him. 'You might get killed—like Dad…'

Oh, sweet heaven. 'Has this been bothering you a lot?'

As if triggered by something he couldn't control, Luke suddenly burst into tears, his small fists pushing hard against his face as he sobbed out, 'If you're gonna be our d-dad—then you shouldn't do dangerous stuff…'

Aiden said nothing, did nothing except hold Luke close until he'd cried himself out. He was shocked at the child's distress, but he, Aiden felt a warmth he never experienced. I can actually be this little kid's dad, he thought in some awe. I can guide him, teach him, befriend him. *Love* him as he deserves to be loved.

After a while, Luke sat up and used the backs of his hands to swipe at his eyes. 'Don't tell Mum I blubbed,' he sniffed.

'It'll be our secret,' Aiden promised. But he

would tell Kate when they were alone. She needed to know she had a son to be proud of.

'About the sky-diving—' Aiden paused. 'I'd already decided not to do it any more.'

Luke looked at him warily. 'H-have you told Mum?'

'Not yet. But I will. I want to keep you safe, Luke. You and Mia and your mum. All of us together. Safe. Always.'

Luke seemed to think there was no further response needed from him. As if shrugging off the whole messy episode, he scrambled up, little gangly arms and legs flying every which-way. Standing, he held out a small fist, touching it to Aiden's larger one in a male-bonding gesture. 'Race you home,' he said with a cocky grin.

CHAPTER TWELVE

IT WAS a week before the wedding. Kate was again in her favourite place on the veranda at Three Oaks.

The seasons were changing. They were heading into spring. A fine time for a wedding, she thought. Everything was going to plan. Family and friends had happily accepted their invitations to share Kate's and Aiden's special day. First at the actual ceremony at the little local church and then here at Three Oaks for what Kate hoped would be the party of a lifetime in celebration of their marriage.

She looked out across the lawn smiling softly. Aiden and her children were there, flying kites. Aiden was pretending to make heavy weather of flying his, his nonsense entertaining Luke and Mia. Kate heard the uninhibited childish laughter, long gurgling giggles, like a stream of soap bubbles.

Aiden was such a part of their lives now, Kate mused. It almost seemed he'd always been there, just waiting until they'd found each other. With that thought, she put her book aside and went to stand at the railings.

Aiden looked up and saw her.

She fluttered a wave.

He wound in his kite.

'Just where did you learn to fly a kite, O'Connor?' Kate sent out the laughing query as he jogged up the steps and stood beside her at the railings.

He cocked an eyebrow. 'You weren't impressed?'

'Uh-uh,' Kate chuckled. 'But you made a lovely clown.'

He opened his arms and she went into them. They held each other loosely. 'You're wonderful with Luke and Mia.' She lifted a hand to trace the outline of his lips.

'They're wonderful kids. And they have a wonderful mother.' Aiden trapped her hand against his chest.

'This time next week, we'll be married.' Kate leaned against him, glorying in the solid strength of his body.

'You'll be on time, won't you?'

'I'll try my best. But if I'm a bit late, you're not to worry. I love you, Aiden.'

He touched a kiss to the side of her throat. 'And I love you, Kate. You're everything I want, everything I need.'

'That sounds like a song,' Kate said and smiled.

'I'll tell you the rest of the words when we're husband and wife.' He sent her the heart-stopping smile that she loved. 'Is everything in place for the reception?'

Kate leaned back in his arms. 'I believe your mum and my mum have everything in hand.'

'So we just have to turn up?'

'Turn up, *married*,' Kate re-phrased softly.

'Oh, yes, that too. I've already given the rings into Brady's safekeeping.'

'He won't forget them, will he?'

'Nah. Jo will see to that.'

'It's going to be such a special day, isn't it?' Kate sighed dreamily.

'Nothing will be as special as when the priest says, "*You may kiss the bride*",' he said huskily, his heart full and light with happiness.

'What about a practice run, then?' Kate responded with a teasing smile. 'We don't want to mess it up.'

'No, we can't have that,' Aiden agreed. 'Not on our wedding day.' He held her close then. Safe against his heart. And kissed her.

* * * * *

Mills & Boon® Large Print Medical

August

SYDNEY HARBOUR HOSPITAL: LILY'S SCANDAL	Marion Lennox
SYDNEY HARBOUR HOSPITAL: ZOE'S BABY	Alison Roberts
GINA'S LITTLE SECRET	Jennifer Taylor
TAMING THE LONE DOC'S HEART	Lucy Clark
THE RUNAWAY NURSE	Dianne Drake
THE BABY WHO SAVED DR CYNICAL	Connie Cox

September

FALLING FOR THE SHEIKH SHE SHOULDN'T	Fiona McArthur
DR CINDERELLA'S MIDNIGHT FLING	Kate Hardy
BROUGHT TOGETHER BY BABY	Margaret McDonagh
ONE MONTH TO BECOME A MUM	Louisa George
SYDNEY HARBOUR HOSPITAL: LUCA'S BAD GIRL	Amy Andrews
THE FIREBRAND WHO UNLOCKED HIS HEART	Anne Fraser

October

GEORGIE'S BIG GREEK WEDDING?	Emily Forbes
THE NURSE'S NOT-SO-SECRET SCANDAL	Wendy S. Marcus
DR RIGHT ALL ALONG	Joanna Neil
SUMMER WITH A FRENCH SURGEON	Margaret Barker
SYDNEY HARBOUR HOSPITAL: TOM'S REDEMPTION	Fiona Lowe
DOCTOR ON HER DOORSTEP	Annie Claydon

November

SYDNEY HARBOUR HOSPITAL: LEXI'S SECRET	Melanie Milburne
WEST WING TO MATERNITY WING!	Scarlet Wilson
DIAMOND RING FOR THE ICE QUEEN	Lucy Clark
NO.1 DAD IN TEXAS	Dianne Drake
THE DANGERS OF DATING YOUR BOSS	Sue MacKay
THE DOCTOR, HIS DAUGHTER AND ME	Leonie Knight

December

SYDNEY HARBOUR HOSPITAL: BELLA'S WISHLIST	Emily Forbes
DOCTOR'S MILE-HIGH FLING	Tina Beckett
HERS FOR ONE NIGHT ONLY?	Carol Marinelli
UNLOCKING THE SURGEON'S HEART	Jessica Matthews
MARRIAGE MIRACLE IN SWALLOWBROOK	Abigail Gordon
CELEBRITY IN BRAXTON FALLS	Judy Campbell

January

SYDNEY HARBOUR HOSPITAL: MARCO'S TEMPTATION	Fiona McArthur
WAKING UP WITH HIS RUNAWAY BRIDE	Louisa George
THE LEGENDARY PLAYBOY SURGEON	Alison Roberts
FALLING FOR HER IMPOSSIBLE BOSS	Alison Roberts
LETTING GO WITH DR RODRIGUEZ	Fiona Lowe
DR TALL, DARK...AND DANGEROUS?	Lynne Marshall

0712 LP 2P P2 Medical